CW00859676

The Missing Half

Brooke Powley

First Edition

Acknowledgements

Many thanks to Christine Rice – editor and general answer to any book related questions.

Special thanks to my beady-eyed proofreaders – Katie Wright and Wayne McClellan.

Thanks to my family and friends who have helped me in this long and sometimes difficult journey of becoming an author.

Last but not least, to Ava – for being yourself.

To Peter – it's your fault this book exists

"In 1996, two-year-old Grace Robinson was taken from her pushchair while her father went into the village shop. Her body has never been found."

Prologue

Alice, 2006

I think I should start by saying that I did not mean for things to turn out this way, and I'm sorry. I'm sorry that you're a stranger to me. I'm sorry that I destroyed your father. Most importantly, I'm sorry that you're gone.

My life has become a spectacle. I have ruined your sister trying to find you. People see me in the street and look twice, recognising my face from TV - or from magazines. I have to hide from the press – pretending to be someone else. Some of them look in pity, some of them in disgust, and the others just stare, not quite knowing what to do or say. I can't even take the children to get new school shoes without people asking questions - *'Did anything ever come of the Mexico tip off?'* Or, the kinder will say, *'She'll come back to you, when the time is right.'*

When I was a little girl and children went missing it was just one of those sad things. It never happened to anyone I knew personally, so it didn't affect my day-to-day life. It happened over breakfast, or lunch. It happened to parents who were *careless*. I knew, in my heart of hearts, that they would never get their little one back. They were sold, or murdered, or raped. I saw the parents on TV, still crying after all those years, pleading for them to return. I continued to eat my cornflakes relatively carefree and thought silently *'let it go... you need to move on with your life'*.

But what would you do, all those years later, when it happens to *you*?

It's been nearly ten years since the day you were taken. My agent tells me that a bestselling book is a good way of refreshing memories, of bringing new evidence to light. The money from the royalties will pay for a team of investigators to follow up on leads, to start afresh on new information, and to troll through everything else – to filter the inaccuracies from the truth.

Hope is twelve now, and she needs to live her own life. I can't keep dragging her with me to 'This Morning' to sit and go over the same old story again and again, – praying that someone out there might be watching, that someone knows something that will bring you back. I want to live a life where I don't have an agent, where people don't recognise my face or worse, your sister's. But I also need to know...what has become of you for all these years? Have you been happy? Loved? Are you worrying about something trivial? Or do you wonder if you really belong?

Grace, I know that I will never be forgiven for my failures as your mother. I've let you down and I won't excuse my behaviour. I do know you are still out there, somewhere. You're not buried in the woods somewhere, or at the bottom of a lake. Of course, every mother of a missing child would say that. I've met several of them over the years, wrapped in guilt; fooling themselves that little Tim is living somewhere nice with a childless couple in Australia. More often than not, little Tim turns up in bits weeks later. But you're different. In all these years, there has never been evidence to suggest you're not still out there. This book is going to bring you back to me. I can feel it.

Part One: Alice

Chapter One

You will be twelve by the time this book is printed, distributed worldwide, and translated into no less than twenty languages. There will be excerpts in newspapers, electronic versions for Kindle, and free posters for every retailer to put in their windows. I wonder how many copies will sell before the tentative link is made and you're brought back to us? I wonder how you will happen across it, or if it will be your next-door neighbour, friend, or librarian, who connects the dots and comes to a conclusion that will bring you home.

It's going to be a long story. I'm sorry about that. I'll try to fill in every little detail however small. That's what the police do when they search for missing children - they take every strand of information, manipulate it, and look at it from every possible angle. It's easier for them though, isn't it? They are just observers. They can go home after a nine-till-five shift to their own nice, happy families, where everyone is present and correct. They can sleep at night when it's someone else's daughter that is missing, or lost, or stolen – a whole range of words that don't capture the pain properly.

If I am going to tell you this story truthfully, it is important to start at the beginning, isn't it? That's what any good investigator would do. I suppose that would take me back to the time when I first met your father.

It happened on a January afternoon when I was twenty-years-old. I had sought refuge in the library, because the house I shared with other students was cold and damp. It was one of those days in which the frost never thaws and the wind is bitter. I was revising for a modular exam on the migration patterns of Grey Whales. It's funny sometimes, the things I remember. Computers were a thing of the future and the internet didn't exist. Libraries, books, and long days pouring over them, was the only way to find the information I needed back then.

Most of the other students were still at home for Christmas break. My father, who was a lecturer in Biology at Cambridge University, had exam papers to mark. My brothers had long since left after the holiday festivities were over, busy with their own lives; Matthew was immersed in his studies and Harry never settled - touring the world, trying to take it all in and decide where he really belonged. All of us were trying to find our own place, which I now realise is common in children who come from tragedy – children who have lost their mother in a cruel twist of fate.

My father tried his best with me, but girls need a mother more than boys. In many ways he suffocated me – by trying to overcompensate, trying to make things right. My father, no doubt, had some guilt because we were motherless, but he led us all well into lives of good education with ambitious dreams for our futures. Following in his footsteps, as a biologist, had led me to Edinburgh University.

Returning to university early from the Christmas break gave me space to breathe. I had seen Jack in the library before, on a handful of occasions. He sat on the far table by the window and tapped his pen in an irritating way. He ate ham and mustard sandwiches for lunch, and he brought a flask of black coffee. I didn't like coffee then, but the smell filled the library in an oddly comforting way.

The day ticked by slowly. The afternoon turned to early evening and other people came and went. I had nowhere else to be, so I loitered a little longer than was necessary. The clock on the far wall next to your father chimed seven o'clock in the evening. I began to return the books that surrounded me to their rightful places on the shelves. The sky outside was dark and the wind was still bitter, but it wasn't much of a walk back to the house from the library, a couple of well-lit streets were no real danger. As I returned the last heavy book to its place, your father had already collected his things and I found him standing by my table.

"Hello," he said. "I thought you might like some company on your way home. It's, well, a bit blustery out there. I'd hate to see you blown away by the wind or held at knifepoint…." He grinned.

"I'm sure that walking home in the dark with a stranger is no less risky than walking on my own," I replied. My house wasn't far off George Square, but I wasn't about to divulge such information to a near stranger. He suddenly whipped his right hand from his pocket and offered it to me, which made me jump.

"Jack Robinson, final year law student. My parents live in York, only child - I've seen you around." He shook my hand rather vigorously.

"Alice Winters," I replied. "From Cambridge originally. Biological Sciences."

"Ahh, that explains a lot.... Women with brains are often well-suited in science! So, now that we are only semi-strangers, I'll walk you home, if only to ease my guilty conscience."

Jack took my bag and we left the library together. I wondered to myself, for a moment, whether his intensions were honourable, while we discussed our various lines of study. He planned to go to London after his graduation - to work for a large firm for a year and complete his training. The pay would be exceptional and he would have an apartment overlooking the Thames. It sounded quite grown-up and serious - a life that I would never want for myself. I told him of my intensions of embarking on a PhD in an area of Marine Biology; though at this point the plans were particularly vague and ambiguous. Unlike other men, he didn't seem enthralled by my plans, which made him even more alluring.

We arrived at my house less than five minutes later. A light was on in the front room and I remembered that my friend Lucy had phoned the evening before to say that she was coming back early.

"Well," he said, "it was nice to speak with you, and I'll be able to sleep now knowing that you weren't mugged on your way home. Perhaps I'll see you again in the library tomorrow?"

I was a little shocked that he didn't invite himself in, and I wondered what the point was in this exercise. I tended to find men more forthcoming.

"Okay. Yes, I suppose that you will."

He placed my bag down on the top step, kissed me quickly - but gently - on my cheek, and left.

I watched him as he walked back down the well-lit road in the wind, and then smiled to myself as I opened the door and went inside to find Lucy. That evening, I let my mind wander to what my father would think of Jack. Would he approve? I was certain that Harry would like him, and it had been a long time since Matthew cared about what I did, silently blaming me for the loss of our mother long before I was old enough to understand.

Looking back, Jack was one of many men who I suppose happened to be studying at Edinburgh University at the same time as me. Later, as we drifted apart, I wondered if I would have given him more than a passing thought if he had served me tea in a café or sat next to me on a train. There had been men before him, but my relationships with them had not been overly significant. One of these men later sold pictures of me to a national newspaper as a scantily clad eighteen-year-old student, which ran aside an article on my 'wild child' days - none of which had much element of truth. Still, he wasn't the first person and I am sure he won't be the last to cash in on another family's pain and misfortune.

I am sure that you have been friends with boys in your time without us, or perhaps at least there have been boys who have been interested in you, who have given you more than a second glance. Hope is quite non-descriptive about such events, preferring to blend in with the crowd and find comfort in girls her own age. She pretends not to be interested in boys. I am sure though, that there have been boys interested in her too.

Do you remember Lucy? She lived with us later at Shell Cottage when you were younger, taking on the role of looking after you and your sister while I finished off my seemingly never-ending PhD.

Anyway, I am beginning to digress. My mind wanders back and forth over the years, over-analysing every little detail - before you were here, after you had gone, and the time we had you with us. I'm sorry about that. This will be a somewhat fragmented rendition of events, but I will try and keep it moving forward as best as I can. You're a bright girl and I'm sure that you will be able to adjust. I'm just sorry that it has to be done like this.

Chapter Two

The following day, the day after your father and I first met, Lucy and I went on a walk up to the castle, and for morning tea at a cosy little that café we frequented together quite often in our student days.

Lucy was studying Psychology and was based in the sciences building from time to time, which was how we had first met and become friends. At this point in time, women, though well-educated, were mostly following careers in History, English and Education. There was always the odd revolutionary woman - Dr Jane Goodall springs to mind - but they were far and few between. I suppose you could say that Lucy and I we were thrown together in another twist of fate, given that we were both bright and had an aptitude for science.

We caught up on each other's events from the holiday season over tea and cake. Lucy always had a string of men following her, or perhaps more that *she* followed, but never a serious kind of boyfriend. The men provide us with much entertainment and deliberation – similar, I imagine, to the way that your sister will chatter on the phone to her friends for hours some evenings. Some of them were quite hopeless, but there were a few good apples among the bunch. The good ones never lasted long though. We often joked that our fathers would relinquish our generous allowances if we got anything less than a first-class honours degree, and so we must focus ourselves back to our studies.

That afternoon, I was keen on getting back to the library and finding your father, after I had somehow promised that I would return. After all, I didn't want him to think that I was being misleading or unreliable. After tea in the café, I stopped at the house to collect my university bag and then walked to the library. It was around half-past-one in the afternoon when I arrived. The campus was still quiet and wouldn't resume its normal business for another week or so. It suited me well, as I could take my time pouring over the reference books, rather than stealing glances at them knowing that many others were waiting for their turn. Jack was sitting at his usual table with his usual flask of coffee.

"Alice!" he said. "I saved you a space. Though, since I've had to fight off unwanted advances from other women all morning you're quite lucky that it isn't taken!" He grinned sheepishly. I realised then for the first time, that he had the most piercing blue eyes that complemented his light-brown hair.

I sat in the empty seat next to him after I retrieved all of the books I needed for the afternoon. We sat there for the rest of the day, stealing glancing at each other from time to time, but mostly focusing on our work. That evening, and every evening thereafter, he walked me back home and we chattered idly, ignoring passers-by, loitering for longer and longer on my doorstep, before it began to become unbearable.

It does sound hopelessly romantic, doesn't it? I wonder if such chivalry is lost in the age of the internet, of countless students never setting foot in libraries, preferring to read journals online, never having to get dressed and wander into the cold outside. It took your father three weeks to ask me out for dinner, and I admit that, by this point, I was becoming rather impatient. During dinner at home, Lucy and I went over and over our wild theories about his lack of interest in food and drink, or even, the cinema. I would tease him about it later - his elusiveness in those early days, when everything was new. Of course, I wouldn't have dared to tread anything but carefully at the time. Inevitably, once he got over his inability to ask for what he wanted, it led to a string of dinners and outings over the following months - the beginning of us, the beginning of you.

Your father remained quite non-committal until he had written his final thesis sometime later in the year, but I had learned enough in the meantime to keep me interested in pursuing him.

Jack's father was a vicar in a small village outside of York, and his mother worked for various charities in the area and volunteered at the maternity unit in the local hospital. Your father had a privileged but strict upbringing, centred round a faith that he mostly resisted. His parents had high expectations for their only son, and he was pushed and expected to go to university to become something important.

I should probably tell you that your grandfather and your father didn't always see eye to eye. They argued about big theological questions; your father simply refused to believe in anything without absolute conviction. Your grandmother, Joyce, was a kinder woman – elegant, poised, and often indifferent to her husband's ideals. It shouldn't make you judge them unfairly though, because all parents and children go through times when they don't agree.

I met them for the first time on the day of your father's graduation, which was about six months after we had first begun dating. *"This is Alice,"* he said to them, *"my girlfriend."* I remember being a bit caught off guard. Though we had been dating exclusively, he'd never referred to me as his girlfriend, and I'd only mentioned him in passing to my own father once or twice. His parents didn't seem to notice. We all sat together during the graduation ceremony, though of course there wasn't a need for much discussion. Afterwards, we went for dinner at an Italian restaurant in town.

Your grandparents were nice enough people, though I felt a rift between us from the beginning. Could a woman from a scientific family ever be at one with a family of faith? Your grandfather on your father's side didn't believe in evolution. In complete contrast of your dad's parents, my father always had a drawing of Darwin above his desk in his office. Medicine and science healed the sick, and religion was a tool people used to make themselves feel better or at least that's what my brothers and I had been told as children.

My father had been involved in some pioneering research on orangutans in Borneo before he met my mother, which is what led him to becoming employed by Cambridge University after they married. After my mother was gone, my father pleaded to have his working hours reduced, mostly because, back then, children were not accepted as full-time boarders until the age of five. Although Matthew was six when I was born, Harry was only two.

In the 1970s, men were not stay-at-home fathers. My father was advised simply to take another wife. Repelled at such an idea, he hired a string of mother's helpers to take care of us while he worked. He didn't work weekends and in the holidays he always worked from home. Harry was kept at home until I was old enough to go to boarding school. When we were old enough, we boarded during the week and came home every weekend.

The summer before school started, our father took a sabbatical from work. He took us trekking in the Indonesian rainforests to see for ourselves, real life apes. For Harry and me, it was a great adventure, but Matthew refused to come with us, and I think that all of us were really relived. Matthew would have been eleven at this point; he chose to stay at school in the holidays, and my father either couldn't or wouldn't force him to do something against his will.

Many years later, after you had gone, the papers hailed this trip as 'reckless' and 'irresponsible'. Ten years after that day, taking such family safari trips was second nature for many people who could afford such luxuries. My father still had a lot of contacts in Indonesia from his days as a young, budding scientist. We travelled with one of his old expedition friends and a group of native minders who knew the areas well and were trained to shoot livestock if we came into any compromising positions. We saw many Asian elephants and Sumatran rhinos but of course, the highlight was seeing the orangutans. At the end of the trip, we spent some time on the coast, watching for whales and dolphins. The marine animals were of great interest to me, and I have no doubt this trip fuelled my need to work as a marine biologist later in my life.

Where was I? Yes - the differences in families and upbringings. As I was saying, our families' ideals were in many ways miles apart. A lot of my family's gripes over God came from the fact that our mother had been taken from us.

Your father's family had never known real tragedy first-hand. It's easier to believe in God if you haven't had your beliefs seriously compromised. I often wondered if your grandfather - on your father's side - would feel differently if your grandmother had been taken from him. I could only speculate how they would have responded to such an event like that, something that was beyond their control.

That summer, after your father's graduation, I took him back to Cambridge to meet my father. Every summer, for the last few years, we had gone out to the South of France and summered in my aunt's villa, which was filled with various members of our family. My aunt was my mother's sister, the last real link we had with my mother's family, since her parents had passed away. I think my father believed that I needed time with a woman, and indeed my Aunt and I had a good relationship. Her daughters - my cousins - were around my age. Now most of them are grown up with children of their own.

Jack was to come out with me to France for a month, before he moved to London. Lucy also joined us for a couple of weeks before we returned to Edinburgh. We spent long summer days doing nothing but wallowing in the sunshine - eventless but not boring. The kind of thing you do when you're footloose and fancy free.

I think my father was sceptical (as any father would be I suppose) of his only daughter embarking in a serious relationship at the age of twenty. He and my mother didn't marry until they were much older. He aired his concerns about me not focusing on my studies, and I assured him that Jack would be too busy working full-time in London and we would be limited to a handful of weekends and holidays. I wondered, really, if this would be the end of us. I imagined that London would be full of young women who might catch his eye, and that it was inevitable that the following year I wouldn't be pursuing a PhD in marine biology in the middle of the capital - the Thames was hardly known for its hub of exciting marine life.

Jack suited his working life. I helped him pick out furniture for his flat, which was near City Hall and overlooked Tower Bridge. The flats were in a rather prestigious building that inevitably was full of other young, working professionals. He paid a thousand pounds extra for his view over the river, which was an extraordinary amount of money back then. We would wander together up and down the riverbanks in the evenings towards St. Katharine's Docks. Often, your father would work late, and we would sit in the living room and just watch the sun go down.

Eventually, the time came for me to return to Edinburgh. Lucy and I moved from the larger damp house into a two-bedroomed cottage, which was much nearer to the university. We both had exams in the first term, and after they were over dissertations to complete. My dissertation focused on the king penguins prolonged breeding patterns, and though I began the research the previous year, I spent a lot of my time up at Edinburgh Zoo researching and collecting data.

Our last year was a real slog. Snatched weekends with Jack became my only respite, and it usually fell on your father to finish early on a Friday afternoon and travel the long train journey to Edinburgh, returning on early Sunday evening, which he loathed. It was the only way. My father said to us when we were younger, *'what doesn't kill you makes you stronger,'* and I suppose that is a fairly accurate representation of where things were then. There were no doubts between Jack and I about doing the right thing, or worries about how our relationship could hurt others around us. Our relationship was growing stronger.

Christmas came and went - Jack and I went home to our respective families instead of spending the holidays together. We spent New Year in Edinburgh with friends, some old and some new.

By January, I had started applying for various PhDs, which were in various parts of the world. My father encouraged me to send applications to the USA and Norway. Though I was still independent, I didn't feel ready to make that jump yet. I also wanted to at least be in the same country as your father. I settled and was readily accepted onto a PhD program based in Cornwall, as part of Warwick University - which was then seen as a bit of a radical institution. My focus would be the cognition and social integration in a group of wild bottlenose dolphins that were living just off the coast of Penzance.

Your father wasn't overly enthusiastic at this news. The train journey to Penzance from London was another long one. In many ways, it would have been easier for him if I had embarked on a project in Norway. Living in London wasn't for me. There would be no real work for me there, and I would have succumbed to being a kept woman. Even later, when you girls were babies and there was certainly enough money for me not to work, the thought of not working repulsed me. I often wonder now how different things could have been if I had been home the day you went missing, if I could have just been that 'kept woman'. The *'what ifs'* are the worst part in this and, of course, there are so many of them.

Graduation became inevitable - after the submission of my final dissertation. Lucy and I began to pack up the year's worth of belongings before our results came by post. Neither of us had cause for concern, as we both graduated top of our respective classes with first-class honours degrees. My father brimmed with pride the day I wore my cap and gown to collect my degree certificate. Harry, and even Matthew, sat with him, though I suspected my father had something to do with that. All of us, including Jack, Lucy, and Lucy's parents, ate an elaborate dinner at a restaurant quite close to the castle. It felt quite sad - the end of an era almost but then, we had new horizons to explore before we became fully fledged adults.

I spent some time back home in Cambridge for a few weeks. Jack was busy working late into the evening, preparing for a big case that was about to go to court, so time with him in London would have been limited. Harry was home too, and we hadn't really spent time together for some years, since we were both at boarding school. We talked about Mathew and his increasing separation from the rest of us, and our father's lack of interest in finding a woman, even though we were all grown up. Just before I headed out to France to my aunt's for my usual summer fix of sunshine, my father summoned me into his office. I was presented with a somewhat astronomical amount of money, in the form of a cheque.

"It's from your mother," my father began. "Her insurance policy paid out after she... moved on. Of course, a lot of the money contributed to three lots of boarding school fees. Matthew and Harry had their own cheques for the same amount at twenty-one. The time didn't seem right for you until now...." He let his voice trail off as if expecting a coherent and well-thought reply. I was, in truth, a bit flabbergasted.

"What am I supposed to... What do I spend it on?!"

"That's up to you. Matthew, I believe, invested most of his. Harry, well he has had a good time with it, if nothing else...." he chuckled to himself "I think, if I were you, I'd invest in property. You're going to be in Cornwall for a few years. You wouldn't lose collateral the way the market is going, and you would also be rent-free and have a place that was really your own."

I thought about Jack and the mortgage he had on his flat in London. It wasn't a sizeable mortgage, given his salary, but he had never been financially helped by his parents, though they certainly had the means to do so. Yet another example of how our families differed. My father made several appointments to view properties with me for when I returned from the summer holidays. I was glad that someone had taken the initiative to sort this out, because I wouldn't really have any idea of where to begin. I was also glad to have some time when I didn't have to think too much about what lay ahead.

Summer, as with all the summers before, came and went too quickly. Your father took some time off work and joined me in France for a short while. His first year was over and he was given a pay rise, but he was still tied to the company for another couple of years. The future impending separation didn't particularly worry me. Your father was, and is, many things, but he was never unfaithful. If things were meant to be, they would work out, and in truth, it wouldn't really be any different from how things had been for us the past year.

Your grandpa and I drove from Cambridge to Cornwall in his car, which I was never allowed to drive, even though I had passed my driving test before I went to University. It was a long and tiresome journey, and we stayed at a hotel in Plymouth for the first evening. My father had a thorough and well-planned itinerary that would keep us busy for two whole days. We looked at various properties in various locations – Penzance, St. Ives, Newquay, Redruth, and St. Agnes. Nothing I saw made me think that I wanted to live there for a long period of time, or particularly excited me to part with large amounts of cash – it was another dreary house in another dreary part of town.

On the very last day we ended up in a small place called Perranporth, quite by accident. We drove down a hill and into the village, parking to the right in a large car park that overlooked the sea front. There were some large cliffs up a steep hill to the right - past the youth hostel - and I beckoned Grandpa up so that we could look out at the views across the beach. We got to the top and the view... well it was just beautiful. Looking from our viewpoint, we could see a lot of Perran Sands, the village, the beach bar and the rock formations.

It was September, so the village was still quite busy, which gave it the feel of a busy seaside place with something for all ages. I could imagine your father and I sitting on the large rock to the mid-left of the beach, watching the tide come in. I could imagine

Lucy and me sitting in the beach bar drinking sangrias in the sun and chatting the night away.

My father gestured to a house set back up the hill a little further on the right, a small garden out front, not too close to the edges of the cliffs. It looked like one of those pictures that a child would bring home from school - two windows on the bottom and two on the top, with a blue door in the middle. There was a large 'for sale' sign outside. Agreeing that it wouldn't hurt to take a look, we walked up to the front door and knocked.

A woman, who must have been in her mid-thirties, opened the door. She explained that the house was quite empty, as the family were emigrating to Australia in a fortnight's time. She gestured us in and led us to the left, through a living/dining room that led to a long galley kitchen and utility room. Back to the right was a larger living room and a downstairs bathroom. The stairs in front of us curved upwards to two bedrooms - a larger one with an en-suite and a smaller one that would easily hold a double bed. In the master bedroom, she used a hook on the end of a wooden pole, to pull down a ladder which led into a large attic room, which she said the owners mostly used as a playroom and storage, but it was wired up to the main electricity and central heating. In the back of the house was a large double garage, garden with apple trees, a patio, and a lawn.

I loved the house. It needed nothing but a good lick of paint all over. The family would be leaving large items of furniture, which were included in the buying price – sofas, dining tables, a washing machine, two double beds, and two single beds. They were in good condition and fairly modern. The buying price was, perhaps, a little more than I wanted to pay, but given that I wouldn't need to buy much furniture, and there weren't or any major decorating issues, it was really ideal. My father suggested putting in a proper stairway to the loft and renting out the spare rooms in the holiday season, which would provide me with extra income for not so much extra work. So it was settled; I offered an amount that was readily accepted, and two weeks later Shell Cottage belonged to me.

I couldn't have known then of the events that would follow. Would you have been taken from us if I had chosen another house? Were your abductors drawn to this pretty seaside town and came across you by complete chance? If I had moved to London to live with your father in his flat, would I be sitting here writing this now?

We still come back to the house - from time to time. Hope puts all of your things - your gifts from over the years, - on your bed, and there they remain, waiting for you to return. Silly isn't it? You will have long outgrown Barbie dolls and rollerblades. I wonder if you will tell us to give them to Oxfam, or put them on E-Bay. You will have had your own gifts from your own 'family'. You probably didn't think about us at all, as you blew out candles on your birthday cake – more likely than not, on a day that would never be your real birthday.

I remained at Shell Cottage for a few years after you were gone, until living there became so unbearable that the attic room was shut off and the whole house became a holiday let. Of course, it isn't known as Shell Cottage anymore. Most people who stay there now don't have any idea that it is the exact same house that was plastered across the major tabloids in the early 1990s. They wouldn't take their children there, if they knew the truth.

We will all return one day, I am sure of it. I will take some time off work and take you both down to Perranporth; we can leave your brother with your stepfather. It won't be long now until you're back with us, where you belong.

Chapter Three

Life in Cornwall seemed to steady me. I enjoyed spending time painting in the house, and Jack and I found a local carpenter to build the stairway to the loft, which gave the house a lot more space. I didn't feel restless, though I probably didn't have time for it. I spent most of the first term in Warwick - gathering resources, attending briefs and meeting with my personal tutor. My studies would begin again properly, as soon as the grip of winter was over, because it would be too difficult to study the dolphins with high winds, icy waters, snow, and unpredictable weather.

We, your father and I, spent Christmas with my father in Cambridge. Harry was home temporarily, and Mathew, by this point, was engaged and spent the holiday with his fiancée's family. My father bought me a Mini, which I thought was the best gift I had ever been given. He muttered something about public transport being unreliable and it not being safe for a young woman of twenty-one to be roaming the streets of Cornwall alone. Reluctantly, we spent New Year with your grandparents. I had really wanted to catch up with Lucy, but Jack insisted it was only fair that we spread our time between both our families.

Working on my PhD began to consume my life. I had no idea that completing a doctorate would take up so much of my time and energy. My waking hours were taken up by research, phone calls and constantly driving back and forth from Perranporth to Penzance to study the dolphins. Your father entered a pattern of working a long week and a Saturday, then taking a long weekend off the following week. He came to Perranporth more than I went to London. It was easier for him to catch a train than it would have been for me to drive. He preferred getting out of the city and escaping to my sleepy seaside village, or at least, that's what I had liked to believe.

The house was coming along well and I had started taking bookings for the two rooms from Easter. Inevitably, this tied me to the house further, as I then had to make breakfasts, wash sheets, and hoover round more thoroughly than I had been doing before.

At that time, I had a PhD bursary from the University, which wasn't a great amount of money, though it was sufficient for food and bills with a little extra left over each month. The money from letting the rooms paid for the upkeep of the house, and covered the times when I'd run low on funds before the bursary had materialised, and helped to pay for expensive equipment I hired when I needed to record the sounds of the dolphins' echoes underwater.

Your father and I became content in life. We holidayed in the winter months when I didn't have many room lettings and was more focused on writing my thesis than watching and recording the pod of dolphins' every movement. We didn't really see much of your father's parents. I suspected that they disapproved of us not being married, of our carefree lives as individuals. I was happy to have them at a bit of a distance. Jack had a good group of lawyer friends in London who he would go out drinking with after work during the week. Mostly, they all had long-term girlfriends. It didn't bother me at the time, but later, when the doubts of life crept in, I wondered why he had remained in London for so long.

Life passed us by for the next twelve months. Matthew was by then married and had moved as far away from us as he could, though he was still in the UK. Harry continued to travel the world. In the summer, Lucy dropped in from time to time to help me out with the house when I had so much work to do for my PhD. I really was burning the candle at both ends. So, in the midst of our busy times you girls took us quite by surprise.

Another Christmas had come and gone, when I began feeling terribly unwell. I put it down to the flu, which eased a little, but I couldn't seem to shake it off. Your father said I spent too much time out in the cold and wet without the right clothing. In mid-February, we went on a trip to Paris. I didn't really want to go, but your father can be quite persistent when he wants to be. *'It'll be fun,'* he would say or *'Well it is already paid for now'*. Paris was, I thought, quite a dreary city.

The Eurostar wasn't invented yet, but it wasn't far off. To get to Paris I had to catch a train to London and from there we would catch a coach, which took us over on the Dover to Calais ferry, before dropping us off in Paris. I don't think your father really understood how ill I was until we were in Paris. I couldn't eat without throwing it back up and tiredness had become a persistent friend. I thought, maybe I was overdoing things again, by having too much work to do and too little time. Jack insisted on travelling back to Perranporth with me afterwards and we would go to the doctors to get to the bottom of what was wrong. By this point, I had lost a good stone in weight and my whole body looked gaunt.

We arrived at the doctors on a Tuesday morning when Jack should have been back at work in London. As I described my illness, the doctor tapped his pen thoughtfully. "When was the date of your last period?" He asked me. I drew a total blank. I looked at Jack. "December? Early December?" I responded, unsure. The pill had never really agreed with me; the coil seemed like an object to fear. I had left contraception up to Jack.

He gave us a pregnancy test to take home – an instant stick-like thing - and a pot to give a urine sample. He told us that severe sickness was possible in many women and that green tea with ginger biscuits may help things to settle. If the doctor's test came back positive, we would be allocated a midwife and an appointment a few days from now. She would take care of things from there.

We wandered home in a state of shock. While I was relieved that I was not about to die from some incurable disease, I wondered, could I really be pregnant? Your father made us a cup of tea while I went to the bathroom to wee on the stick. When I was done, I placed the stick on the dining room table, took my tea, and sat down next to Jack of the sofa.

"The line needs to be pink - it says to wait five minutes," I explained to him. I knew how the tests worked. I knew that human pregnancy tests worked well on gorillas and that many zoos used them to confirm a gorilla pregnancy. You pick up many bits of useless animal facts when your father lives and breathes them. I had never envisaged taking one myself for another good few years.

It was Jack who eventually got up to look at the stick. He sat next to me and put it in front of me. The line was most definitely - pink. Your father seemed to be grinning. I suddenly burst into uncontrollable tears.

"Alice," he said to me, "nothing has changed. I still love you. I'm still in love with you. I know we are young and we don't live together right now, and things are... - far from ideal. Things will be okay; everything will be okay. You don't need to worry."

By this point, I was beyond capable of being able to construct a proper sentence. I let him wipe the tears from my face. I must admit that I did have doubts. How would we manage? How could Jack go on working in London? How would I finish my studies? Your father was good in a crisis. He took a week off from work, tidied the house, and brought me poached eggs in bed. He talked about painting the spare room, and buying a cot, and of when was an appropriate time to tell our parents. I quite enjoyed having him around. It was as if his positive attitude cancelled out my worries, or at least most of them.

Jack pulled some strings to get an appointment with an ultrasound technician later that week before he would go back to London. We travelled to Newquay in my little Mini without too much trauma. Newquay had a smaller hospital with an outpatient department and a few wards, including a midwife-led maternity unit. There was a bigger hospital at Truro that dealt with pregnancies that are more complicated. The hospital seemed like a big scary place, but Jack took it all in his stride. There seemed to be a lot of older couples in the waiting room. I was told to drink a lot of water to enhance the scan quality and I honestly thought I was going to wet myself at any moment.

The woman squeezed the jelly over my tummy, while Jack sat on the chair next to me, taking my left hand, and looking at the screen. She found what looked instantly like a baby and said,

"Well, it seems like you stopped on buy-one-get-one-free day. You have twins and they both look strong and healthy." She moved the screen outwards a little and there on the screen were two little, perfectly beating hearts.

*

Given that we hadn't, at this point, told anyone we were expecting, let alone twins, there came a flurry of excitement and panic. There were logistics to work out with your father's job; he was looking instead at commuting to Exeter and renting out his flat in London to cover the mortgage and any repairs that it would need. With two babies in the house, it would be difficult to rent out the rooms in my cottage. I applied for planning permission to turn the double garage into a self-contained apartment. It would be less work for me to just change beds and the money from the apartment would go towards paying someone to help with the babies when I eventually go back to work to finish my studies.

My father wasn't exactly enthralled at the prospect of becoming a grandfather, which, in hindsight, wasn't surprising given that I was twenty-three and Jack twenty-five at the time. Still, he adjusted to it, with time.

Jack's parents were thrilled. His mother phoned every day to ask what was going on, and sent matching knitted hats, gloves, cardigans, and booties in the post every week until you both arrived.

I busied myself with work most of the time, eager to get ahead and for pregnancy not to hinder my studies. I worried a lot about how things would work out. I suppose that's inevitable for any first-time expectant mother of twins, but for me the fear was intensified due to the loss of my own mother – the mother who I had never really known. I went to every doctor's appointment, read every little piece of paper on pregnancy, and did everything by the book, but the negative thoughts of disaster were never far from mind. Your father said I was being silly. *'No one dies in childbirth anymore, Alice.'* On an intelligent level, I knew he was right, yet I thought of all those women in Africa or Brazil who died everyday due to improper medical care. What if something went wrong? How would Jack ever manage working full-time with two babies to care for?

My father arrived in Perranporth over the Easter holidays. I knew he had come to talk to me about my mother. I imagined Jack speaking with him on the phone, telling him that I was overreacting. I imagined my father telling him that overreacting was a perfectly reasonable response to my situation given the circumstances, but that he would find time to come down and talk to me. I took him over to Penzance several times, showed him my study and the pod of dolphins who tailed my boat when we went out to sea. My findings weren't yet conclusive, but I had a good idea of how to wrap things up with more of the right data.

We ate at the local pub most evenings. The beach bar was just open for the tourist season, but trawling across the sand in the rain, and looking out to the sea in the mist, would spoil the atmosphere. Predictably, it was on the last evening when he broached the subject. Talking about my mother had never been one of his strong points. I think that his pain of losing her was too great.

"Alice," he said to me, "I can see that you are worried about the twins." He looked at me, waiting for my acknowledgement. I nodded my head - cautiously.

"Your mother was a great woman, Alice. But she was a lot older than you are now when we were considering having children. The boys were straightforward pregnancies followed by easy home births. It's what most women did then - midwives were trained well and doctors were called in emergencies. When she fell pregnant with you, I thought it was too soon after Harry. He was barely a year old and she had Matthew at home too, without any help; though we could have easily afforded it, she didn't want it. With you though, she was more tired, more sick. She was insistent that you would be born at home. I had an uneasy feeling, but your mother was quite good at getting things her way. The midwife said her placenta was a little low but nothing to worry about. You were born quickly, too quickly. By the time it was obvious that something was wrong it was too late. You were lying on her chest as she was bleeding out. She was semi-conscious. She told me you were to be called Alice, after her mother. The ambulance didn't arrive in time... and then she was gone..."

I wiped tears from my eyes. I had known the basic story for most of my life, given to me in bits over the years from various family members. My mother wanted to give birth at home, and it just went wrong. I remember my anger at her as a teenager. Why hadn't she listened? Why didn't she go to the hospital as my father had pleaded? In one respect, maybe you don't miss what you never had. Her pictures are still all over the house, but she was all but a stranger to me. When my brother and I were little, my father would mention our mother in passing, like as an old lost friend. Harry and I were too young to understand.

"Matthew blamed you, because you were an easy target. He had always been his mother's boy. I worked longer hours when he was younger and I spent more time away. He accepted Harry, Matthew was in nursery by then. Harry didn't impede on his time with his mother. When she was gone, he just shut down. No one was good enough. I couldn't reach him; he blamed me almost as much as he blamed you. He was just a boy ... he didn't really mean it. I should have tried harder. I should have got him proper help. I should have insisted that it wasn't your fault. Every day after, I kicked myself in anger. Alice, what happened to your mother was terrible. But times have changed and things will be different for you. You have choices and you have the whole world at your feet."

I felt a weight lift from my shoulders. My father was right; I had spent many years believing that I was responsible for my mother's death. I wondered how he coped, with three young children and his own guilt. I thought about Jack and his insistence that the twins would be fine, that a natural birth at a midwife led unit was safe. Doctors would be on-call if something happened. I just had to believe. Sounds so simple doesn't it?

The later stages of pregnancy were difficult. You were due at the end of October, but multiple babies often come a couple of weeks sooner – something about too many babies and too little space. The garage was finished and was booked up with various families for the whole summer. Although I had told my father I would ease off with letting out rooms in the house, I was still letting the two spare rooms towards the end of my pregnancy. The people next door had a teenage daughter, Rosie, who came over a few mornings every week to clean. Your father would be moving to an office in Exeter in September and would commute from Perranporth in his car. His flat had been let to someone who was moving into his old office. Everything had come together well.

Your grandparents had come down from York just before the birth. I was sceptical of having them living in our house with two babies, but I didn't have the heart to ask them to stay in the new self-contained apartment. Jack insisted that they would be useful. He wouldn't have a lot of time off work and I would need help, someone to cook at least.

At thirty-six weeks pregnant, the decision of having a natural birth was taken out of our hands. My blood pressure had been elevated for a while and wouldn't come down. I was being scanned every two weeks to monitor the progress and one of you wasn't growing enough. The consultant recommended a caesarean. I was torn between relief of not having to go through a natural birth and anger at not even being able to try. On the 28th of September 1993, I was wheeled into surgery.

Chapter Four

Before I had you, I heard many women proclaiming that having a child was the day that transformed their lives. In Antenatal class, we were shown breathing techniques, pictures of babies in vitro at certain ages, and a doll being pushed through a woman's pelvis. Caesarean was mentioned in passing and was no doubt portrayed as the easier option. It's not surprising that I, therefore, found the experience fairly traumatic.

I felt an odd tugging sensation as the consultant made an incision in my stomach to retrieve you both. You came first, Grace, our first daughter. Six pounds and two ounces with fair hair and a belting cry. They gave you to your father and we stared at you, quite amazed, while they retrieved your sister. She was pulled out a mere forty seconds later, in what can only be described as a blind panic. They whisked her away quickly and I couldn't see what they were doing or what was going on.

"It isn't crying... Why isn't it crying? - Is it..." I looked down at you, our one healthy, perfect daughter, not at all squashed like some of the babies we saw in those Antenatal videos who had to squeeze their way down the birth canal. We thought we had lost your sister. It must only have been mere seconds in the flurry of panic before your sister let out a deafening cry. My heart felt immediate relief.

Hope was a little smaller than you at five pounds six ounces. As they brought her over and placed her right next to you, the similarities were remarkable. We knew that you would be identical before the birth. But we didn't know if you would be boys or girls because your father wanted a surprise. Identical twins of different sexes are possible but exceedingly rare. He thought we would have two boys – Charlie and Frankie. Would he have been more careful with two boys? Instead, while they were stitching me up, you became Grace and Hope. Grace was the name of my mother, and Hope was the surname of the surgeon who delivered you. Your last names would be Robinson and not Winters, or Robinson-Winters. There was no need to cloud the issue.

The staff in the hospital put me onto a ward that had two other mothers, both with single babies and both a little older than me. I had to wait for the epidural to wear off before I could walk around. Getting up and down was quite difficult. The midwives encouraged me to breastfeed you both. They fed us vast amounts of food and snacks on demand, which I would eat hungrily as if I had never been fed before. I was determined to try and do everything right and was running on adrenaline for the first day or so. Your father often sat beside my bed and simply watched your chests rise and fall. We took turns holding each of you, in those early days when we hadn't quite managed the art of being able to hold you both at once.

The first night, they sent your father home and left me alone with you both. At around eight o' clock in the evening, the midwife came round and told me to feed you girls, and then she would take you both to the nursery so that I could get some rest. She would bring you or your sister back when you needed feeding. I slept for six glorious hours. No one had returned with you, so I wandered to the midwife station. I saw you both, lying there side by side and sound asleep. I sat and watched you before the midwife shooed me away insisting I needed rest.

We had no visitors for three days. Your father came prompt every morning and was politely shown the door at eight every evening. We bathed you, changed you, and tried to work out how we would ever tell you apart at home. The grandparents came to visit you first, who adored you. Harry and Lucy arrived together, bringing gifts and cards and balloons – two of everything, matching and pink.

After a week, I began to want to be back at home. Your father had three weeks off work, which was unheard of then for parental leave. The midwives would visit daily since you girls were born a little early, I had had a c-section, and of course, there were two of you. The day that we brought you home, your father wrote each of your initials on a soft yellow ribbon and tied them to your ankles. It took us a while to be able to tell you apart properly and it worried me that we would mix you up once the hospital bands had been cut.

Having you home was wonderful. We didn't do a lot in those early days before your father went back to work. Your grandparents moved into the apartment in the garage and they cooked and cleaned. I breastfed you both when you were hungry. Jack would take you both out in the double pushchair for two hours every afternoon while I caught up on sleep. It would be another few weeks before I could manage pushing you both up the steep hill from the beach to Shell Cottage.

When you were three-weeks-old, your father went back to work and I was a little shocked at having to manage you both without him there. Of course, your grandparents were still around and still cooked meals so I didn't have to cook or clean. When they went back to their own home a week later, I was left in utter despair. I dared not leave the house, and I handed your father both of you as soon as he walked through the door. Dinner was rarely cooked, and the house... well let's just say it wasn't being cleaned either.

Those early days of non-stop feeding and one of you crying every five minutes, didn't last long. But those days were exhausting, both mentally and physically. Rosie, from next door, who, at fourteen, came over and helped me clean, was besotted with you girls. I paid her to come over a couple of nights after school and on Saturdays, which allowed me to spend time with each of you individually without feeling guilty.

You both grew into beautiful and happy little girls. You slept well at night, and you didn't make too much fuss. Hope was the first to sit up but you, Grace, were the first to crawl. Your father had to put up baby gates all over the house to stop you from escaping. Just before you were six-months-old the prospect of me needing to get back out with the dolphins was looming, I devised a plan. Lucy by this point was at a bit of a loose end, between jobs with nowhere really to stay. I persuaded her to come and live with us rent free, so long as she helped with you girls each morning, so that I could go out and continue to gather my data on the dolphins. Your father wasn't overly enthusiastic about the idea, but he was easily persuaded. The apartment was booked for the whole of the summer holidays and there was no way I could have managed you both, study and the upkeep of the apartment.

Life had shifted again. I missed you girls when I began working with the dolphins, but I was glad for a little bit of time to myself. We did more in the afternoons, as I felt guilty for leaving you at home with someone else. I completed my writing up in the evenings while you were sleeping. Lucy encouraged me to go to the local toddler group. She took you every Tuesday morning and insisted that the women weren't middle-aged dragons who swanned around town with their designer handbags. So I started taking you to the village hall and chatted with other mothers over tea while the children played amongst the toys. I struck a particular friendship with a woman called Jane, probably the only woman I still hear from now who I knew from back then. She had a little girl, Poppy, who was the same age as you girls. She invited us round for lunch and had you both for play dates when you were a bit bigger. It is a shame really, that we drifted apart over the years.

Lucy was a real great help around the house and I loved having her around. It made me feel like I wasn't completely alone. Your father left early every day and returned late. He was home for weekends, but that was when I was often working, squeezing in my time when I knew he would be around to look after you both. I suppose that's what happens to all newborn parents - they inevitably drift apart. We adored you both and you were our common ground, but we began to have quite different lives.

Your first birthday came and went. You were both walking and chatting away. We went on trips to the beach for long, lazy summer afternoons and had picnics after I had returned from my morning's work over in Penzance. You were happy playing in the sand, but Hope was happier by the water. We took our fishing nets to the rock pools and searched for crabs. We came home covered in sand, with rosy cheeks. You girls fell into your beds exhausted, and Lucy and I would sit lazily in the front garden with a gin and tonic.

That winter of 1994 was cold and bitter. It rained nonstop, and there were a lot of houses in the village that flooded due to the raging high tides. Lucy and I decorated the attic after the workmen put in more windows to make it lighter inside during the day. It was a huge open space and it became your bedroom/playroom.

Lucy was going to be heading off to Australia for a while - to do some work in a private Psychology clinic. As it was winter, and I was so close to finishing writing up my PhD, I put you girls into the local private day nursery for three mornings a week. The nursery was in the village and you both loved it. Your father moaned to me about the expense, but I didn't see it as a major problem.

That year, we all spent Christmas together at Shell Cottage. Jack had some time off work and we talked about taking some time away together on holiday before the tourists came back to Perranporth. Jack booked us into a hotel in Lanzarote that May. It was the first trip you had ever taken abroad. I was nervous about taking both of you with no one else to help. It sounds silly, doesn't it? I was used to having Lucy with me most of the time. Sometimes I'd have you both for an afternoon or a morning, but not all the time. It's difficult to do things with two young toddlers and I worried about dangers like the water. You were both blonde, which made you harder to spot in a crowd, and Hope was prone to wandering. Had I thought about one of you being abducted? Of course, it crossed my mind. Your father said I worried too much about it all instead of enjoying the moment. It came back to haunt him later, but we are another year away from that yet.

So off we went, armed with sun cream and bags full of stuff. We had two glorious weeks. We took you to the pool every day and we went out to dinner, before returning and putting you to bed in our little apartment. You had a double pushchair, which was supposed to fit through a single door but of course, it didn't. I could manoeuvre it into shops adeptly, but your father struggled, as he never took you into shops at home but would push you around at the park or on the beach. If we stayed out a little later than we should have, you both would fall asleep and we would enjoy the rest of the evening.

We needed that holiday, your father and I. We talked about the things that niggled us. Your father didn't want you in the private day nursery so much, which would never be possible if he continued to work in excess of sixty hours a week. He agreed to spend two mornings a week at home with you both and then work on a Saturday. We talked about Rosie, our sweet teenage neighbour, and how really she could cope with both of you on a Saturday morning while I went to work. After all, her parents lived next door and I was half-an-hour away in case of an emergency. Sundays come rain or shine; we would all do things together – family day.

Our new routine worked very well. Eventually, I pulled you both out of the private nursery, as you were both happy playing together and I could get a fair amount of things done with you both at home with me. The last summer we had you with us, we spent a lot of time outside in the sun. Rosie came with us on various excursions and you both liked visiting the dolphins.

My thesis was pretty much completed and I was waiting to hear if I had to make any changes to it before submitting officially. Warwick University approached me with an offer of a reasonable salary to become a mentor for the next round of PhD students who would be coming to pursue further lines of study with the pod. It would allow me to have more time at home, but would also allow me to continue to spend time with fellow researchers and to pass on the wealth of knowledge about the pod I had acquired myself. In many ways, they dolphins felt like my second family.

That winter was not as bitter as the previous. Your second birthday had come and gone, marked with a small party on the beach with some of your toddler group friends. Your last Christmas with us was happy and non-eventful. Again, all the family came down to Shell Cottage and we over indulged in food and wine alongside the rest of the nation.

Your father and I went away to Edinburgh for New Year on our own. It was the first - and last - time we were away from you for more than a few hours. We had a wonderful time celebrating Hogmanay with our old university friends. Your father wanted us to have another baby, but I was quite unsure. I felt that you had both become a nice age in which we could really enjoy doing things together as a family. A baby would tie us down further, and you two were barely two-years-old. Three toddlers under the age of three seemed like an impossibility.

Later, I wondered silently, if I had been pregnant again on the day you were taken, it is unlikely that you would have ever been out of the house at all – I'd have been too pregnant to be out on a boat in unsteady waters. But of course, it's all speculation, isn't it? I mean, I was sick as a dog when I was pregnant with you two, but there is no real guarantee that the same would happen again. I persuaded your father that we should wait to have another baby until you were three-and-a-half when you both would have been off at nursery together and there would have been a little more time for me to take care of a new baby, or rather, more time for me to manage a new baby with two toddlers. Amidst the discussions, we both felt it was right to cut our trip short by a day and come back early to you girls - to enjoy the time we had free from our work commitments with you both.

I submitted my thesis six weeks after New Year, after a stint of hard work at home. I officially became a doctor the week before you were gone. The papers always ran my name as Alice Robinson, which was wrong; since your father and I never married, much to your grandparents' dismay. It was then that I began to use my professional name - Dr. Alice Winters.

It is so hard for me to recall the days around that awful day you were taken from us. It's going to be hard for you to read about it too. There are so many things I kicked myself for after it happened, that kept me awake night after night.

Hindsight can be a glorious thing. I couldn't have known it was going to happen - you must know that? Every morning since I have woken up and wished, wished that I hadn't insisted your father take you both while I nipped over to Penzance. I didn't really need to be there that day, rallying up my PhD students; they had time to make their own mistakes. I didn't need to be there, making sure they did things right. I should have been at home.

I have re-lived that day over and over and over, until, sometimes I wonder what is my own memory, what is a newsflash, and what is evidence given to me in drips and drabs over the years by the police or private investigators.

So many things that I didn't even consider, that various people had me answer over again and over in those early hours and days, every detail significant, important, and needing to be logged. Were you both well? Why did you, Grace, always sit on the left side of the pushchair? Why were you more sleepy than usual? Had you been given calpol? Were you running a temperature? Did we receive any strange phone calls? Were there any longer-than-is-appropriate glances at the twins? Were we suspicious of being followed?

Every moment in the days leading up to your disappearance were checked, double checked, and verified by independent witnesses - as if we couldn't be trusted. We failed you though, didn't we? You were taken and we were the only people to blame.

I'm sorry that this will be difficult for you, Grace. It will be difficult for me too. But it is important, isn't it? It's important for you to know. It's important for other people to dig deep and think about all the unanswered questions. It's important to find the answers to your disappearance. We can do it; we can do it if it means that you will come home.

Chapter Five

A month before you were taken, a man walked into a primary school gymnasium and shot a class of children - most of them only five-years-old, before he killed himself. It happened in a small village in Scotland. Four days before you were gone, they knocked the entire school down. Later, I understood the pain that could be associated with a building first hand. They couldn't look at it, couldn't enter it. There wouldn't ever be any chance of happy memories after such a tragic loss.

Three days before you were taken was a Friday. It was an ordinary Friday; your father was at work and I was at home with you both all day. I took you to playgroup in the morning and chatted with Jane about the mundane issues surrounding our lives – that I would be taking you for new shoes the following week, Poppy's lack of interest in potty training and who was going to run in the local elections in May.

That afternoon I took you both to Morrison's in Newquay to do some food shopping. Shopping with you both at almost two-and-a-half was tricky. Usually, we went on a Saturday afternoon with Rosie and she entertained one of you at a time while the other was in the trolley, or better still, we would have two trolleys. That afternoon you were both chatting away as we went round the supermarket. You, Grace, were in the trolley, and Hope was walking by the side. You were happier sitting in pushchairs, car seats or trolleys - more so than Hope. You liked to look at all the people and see what they were up to.

Halfway round we came across a man in the tinned aisle. He struck me as a bit odd at first glance - a bit shabby, with dark hair poking out of a woollen hat, and brown eyes.

"Pretty girls," he said to me, as Hope reached for tins of beans and put them in our trolley. "So many people wanting pretty girls now. It must be hard to have two." He had an accent - European? Polish? Greek? He made me feel uncomfortable. I smiled weakly. I put Hope in the trolley next to you, which was a squeeze and she wriggled impatiently.

I raced round the rest of Morrison's as if it were an episode of Supermarket Sweep. I paid and we left without any major occurrence. Who was that man? I am sure he had something to do with you being taken. The police couldn't trace him later. Did he know that I was going to go shopping? Were we followed? Did he see you that day and decide that he wanted to have one of you, or both? Did he make assumptions about my tiredness, my hair thrown into a bobble, my lack of makeup, and think you were better off with someone else? Someone richer? Someone with no children at all?

We got back home and I unloaded the shopping. You girls were happy, playing in the back garden, which was fenced off and secure. I sat and watched you play while I read my book intermittently. I chatted with Rosie's mum, who had popped round for a cup of tea. Rosie was doing her GCSEs and wanted to go to college to study childcare the following September. I couldn't imagine her doing anything else than doting on other people's children, but her mother wasn't so sure about it all.

Your father returned home at just after seven. You were both ready for bed and your father took you up to your room just after seven-thirty to put you down for the night. As we had dinner, pasta, I didn't mention the man in Morrison's. I knew that your father would say it was silly, that I was jumping the gun or worrying about nothing. It wasn't nothing though, was it, Grace? It wasn't nothing.

Two days before you were gone was a Saturday. On Saturday mornings I was still going out to Penzance to work with my group of PhD students. As I mentioned earlier, I was now Dr. Winters, but I still wanted to carry on; I wanted my students to have the passion for work that I did.

Rosie arrived at eight a.m. that Saturday and was with you both until I returned at twelve.

In Penzance, two of my students were eagerly waiting. They were going through the early stages of learning to tell the dolphins apart, something I'd had to do alone and that took up a great deal of time before I could begin any of my research.

Rosie took you both to the park at about 10:30 am, and pushed you in the pushchair round the back road. You were at the park for about forty-five minutes in total. Rosie saw on odd-looking woman sitting on a bench reading a book. She had no children, red hair, and pale skin. She didn't speak or make a scene, and she seemed to be watching the comings and goings of people at the park.

Later, when this was reported to the police in the routine enquiry, they would also fail to trace her. Was she significant, or was this coincidental? Was she somehow related to the man in Morrison's? Why had she never been traced? Two strange people in a matter of days, but of course, on that Saturday, the woman was so insignificant that Rosie didn't even mention it to me when I returned at 11:45am.

That afternoon, after we had lunch, your father returned home at around one o'-clock. Rosie had gone home for a few hours to study as Jack and I were going out that evening for dinner with Jane and her husband. We took you down to the beach for a little while. You ran around together, barefoot in the sand, while holding hands, as you looked out on the sea and dared to edge your feet a little closer to the cold water in the April sunshine. You, Grace, looked out towards the sea from our spot on the beach, – watching the tide in your pink cotton dress.

The pictures we took that afternoon are the last pictures we have of you together. The papers would run articles with the pictures in occasionally but as most of them didn't show your faces, they weren't used as much as the others. I wonder if you have seen them? We have the picture of the both of you - printed onto a poster and framed, hanging in the hall where we hang our coats. Every day, twice a day, we all see it, as we hang and retrieve our items. Just because you're not with us now, doesn't mean we don't remember.

In the evening, we put you both to bed before Rosie came to babysit. You both usually slept all night long. It was rare if one of you woke up, though it did happen occasionally. There was a charity event at the local pub. It seemed a good excuse to mingle a bit with the locals we had come to know. I was looking forward to spending time out on our own in the village. We previously planned that if we went out for an evening, we would call at ten from a payphone to make sure that everything was okay. If there was ever a problem, Rosie would call the pub and one, or both, of us would come back. We returned at about eleven-thirty. Jack walked Rosie back next door. We didn't stay up much later than twelve.

Your last full day with us was family day, Sunday. Ironic, really, isn't it? We all went swimming in Newquay. Swimming was one of those things that I couldn't really manage with you both on my own. The pool was always warm and you girls liked to take turns going down the slides; we usually got more than our monies' worth.

Afterwards, we all went and had fish and chips at a little café on the front. You girls were good eaters, and you liked fish. We had been to this particular café before, and nothing was unusual or odd that day. After we had eaten, we walked together to the bookshop. It had become a habit that if we ended up in Newquay we would buy each of you a book. You both loved to read - or at least, look at the bright colourful pictures.

We drove home along the coast and you both had a short nap. That afternoon we made some fairy cakes, which used up the last of the eggs. Somehow, in the panic of the odd man, I had forgotten to buy some in Morrison's. By now, it was just past four in the afternoon, and the local village store would be shut. I liked to have a boiled egg for breakfast on most mornings.

Sometimes I think that's what all of this comes down to - my love of boiled eggs and my inability to cope without them. I mentioned to Jack that we needed more eggs, because it would be him who ended up at the village shop the next morning to buy them. If it is any consolation, I no longer eat anything the same for breakfast and certainly not eggs. But it isn't much consolation really, is it? It never will be.

Rosie's mother called at around six-thirty, while I was in the front room with you both trying to persuade you two to get ready for bed.

"Rosie won't be able to make it in the morning," your father informed me. "Her mother thinks she has tonsillitis – she has a raging temperature. We better keep an eye on the girls."

"I was really hoping to get out on the boat...Shall I call the nursery? Maybe the girls can go there for a few hours...."

"No. I'll work it out. I can work late on Friday. But you must be back for twelve, as it will take me longer to get into the office mid-day."

Your father didn't like the nursery. I suspected he didn't want to reorganise his work schedule either, but as I have already told you several times, I was insistent on going to Penzance. Looking back, it was as if a pod of wild dolphins were more important to me than my own family, my own daughters. Nothing more was said on the matter that evening and so it was settled.

There were no strange people to report on day three, or if there were, neither your father nor I noticed them. I took you both upstairs at seven-thirty and tucked you into bed, as I did every single night. I drew the curtains. I told you that I loved you. I turned off your light.

Chapter Six

On Monday, 15th of April at 6:45am it was I who awoke first. I jumped in the shower while your father went to make himself a coffee. Twenty minutes later I joined him in the kitchen. I ate a banana from the fruit bowl. Your father laughed as he ate his toast and cereal. He knew that I'd rather hold out for my eggs than have something that I didn't really want. I'd be back in four-and-a-half hours. I kissed your father on the cheek before I left. You were both still sleeping. I didn't go upstairs to see you before I left, as I often did. I didn't even say goodbye.

At seven-thirty, I left the house and drove over to Penzance. It was a clear morning and we went out on the boat. The dolphins were lively. We moored in a little part of the coast and literally sat and watched them for hours. The students were getting much better at identifying them as individuals. It was important for them to be able to do this before they could each begin their data collection.

At home, your father went upstairs to check on you at eight-fifteen. You were both awake by then. You both liked playing with your toys for a little while before breakfast, so it's probable you had been awake since around eight. He brought you both down to the dining room and sat you at the table. For your breakfast, you both ate Weetabix and toast. By nine- thirty, you were both dressed in denim dungarees with a white t-shirt underneath and a navy cardigan on top. The weather was warm, so your father put your coats in the bottom of the pushchair. You were both wearing brown leather Clarks shoes, that had a silver buckle.

At ten-o'clock, he got you both and put you in your double pushchair to take you for a short walk before going to the small village shop for his paper - and the eggs that I wanted.

I wished we had gotten rid of that pushchair. Your father was more apt than I was at pushing it around the place, but he found it difficult to get it into a single shop door, even though it was supposed to be able. It was a tricky manoeuvre, and of course, once you were inside, you had to leave it by the door anyway, and people would look in a disapproving way because it took up so much space. Later, there would be all kinds of double pushchairs that would glide through doors with ease. Later for you though, was simply too late.

Your father walked you both round the village. You took some bread to feed the ducks that would often come to the boating lake. You had your little toy penguin with you, and since it had become your favourite; it rarely left your side.

As you neared the shop, your father noticed that you, Grace, had fallen asleep. Since he was only nipping in for half-a-dozen eggs and a paper, he took Hope out of the pushchair, who was awake, and angled you to a position in which - he thought - he could still see you. There weren't many people around that day, but it was still early – between 10:43 and 10:46. That's the official amount of time your father was in the shop, since we had better be precise with the police report. He left you out there for those three precious minutes, while he got the shopping and chatted to John - the man who ran the shop with his wife. Quite simply, by the time he had returned, you were gone.

Instead of going back into the shop and asking in a calm and rational way for John to phone the police (the police would later say this is what a parent should have done in this situation), your father shouted your name and ran, with Hope in his arms, to the seafront. You were nowhere to be seen. He grabbed a passer-by - a tourist, we would later learn.

"Have you seen my daughter, Grace? I can't find her! She is two, with blonde hair…." He thrust Hope in the woman's face. "She looks just like this – they're twins." The woman shook her head.

Your father ran back to the shop, half expecting you to be standing there waiting. But why would you have been, logically? You were fastened into the pushchair when your father went in and you couldn't have undone the straps yourself. He barged through the door this time and John was serving another local.

"Phone the police, John, quickly. It's Grace. She's…she isn't in her pushchair. We need to find her. I need to find her." He practically threw Hope at John while he fled the scene, running to the boating lake, the playground, the house, and Poppy's.

In the twenty minutes your father frantically searched the village for you, the police had arrived at the shop. John had used his initiative to call the coastguard, knowing that I was out on the boat. We got a radio message that I should come back straight away. I was already speeding my way back through to Perranporth - what should have been a good half-an-hour's journey.

The police officer was sent from the small station up on Liskey hill. Your father, who had calmed down a little and was beginning to look at this a bit more rationally, explained to him what had happened - that you had been taken while you were sleeping in your pushchair outside the shop less than an hour ago.

"She probably just wandered off," was the officers' response, "but we will take you down to the station for a formal statement and will call in more officers to have a good look around the village"

"I've already looked in the obvious places. Someone has taken her. We need traffic reports and pictures on the news; we need to make the ferries aware of what is going on."

Your father told me that the police officer looked at him as if he were a raging lunatic. Two-year-old girls did not go missing in Perranporth, and if they ever had in the past, they were never the subject of a national missing persons' campaign, which is what you would become.

I arrived at the shop precisely one hour after you had been taken. Hope brightened as she saw me. John had given her some paper and pencils to occupy her and found her a space in the back room. Your father was a complete bundle of nerves. I had never seen him in such a flap before; he was usually so calm in a crisis. It didn't dawn on me then, that we would never get you back; but I was worried and anxious for you to return.

The policeman made a catalogue of errors that day that would come to light over the next few days – the shop was not cordoned off, I wasn't interviewed officially at all that day, pictures were not circulated in the right way at the right time, and passport control was not alerted at all. But the worst thing of all was the policeman who told me to take Hope home - in the same pushchair that you had been taken from, before it had been examined by forensics. Any chance of finding your abductor was lost in that instant. I'm ashamed to say that I didn't think about it either, as I walked Hope back up the hill, but I feel less guilty about that now. I wasn't a trained police officer. My first thoughts weren't about forensic evidence, but about having my little girl back, safe, where she belonged.

I made cheese on toast for lunch, which Hope ate greedily but I couldn't touch at all. I couldn't even stomach the thought of eating until you were brought back, which would surely only be a matter of hours, I guessed.

Your sister played with some books in the living room awkwardly. It was rare for you girls to be separate, though it happened more frequently now that you were older and had different demands. At this time, she hadn't asked where you had gone and I certainly couldn't have begun to explain it to her. It was as if she understood something serious was happening and it was better if she sat tight and rode it out like the rest of us.

From the window in the living room, I could see that the village was full of police – three cars in the main car park and several on foot, stopping passers-by. I phoned my father and he insisted on travelling down straight away. The only thing that I remember him telling me clearly was that he would phone his friend who worked for the BBC, because if you hadn't been returned by five o'clock, we would need to prepare for the six o'clock news. I couldn't even think a few hours ahead, and I certainly didn't want to imagine that you wouldn't be back with us for dinner - when I imagined we would all sit laughing about your misadventure.

Your father returned home just after one. For now, his interview was over. He called John at the shop to thank him for his help in alerting the police so quickly. Someone more official at the station told him the first few hours were critical and the best thing we could do was sit at home and wait while the police conducted a 'thorough' search of the local area. Jack began to ring round people we knew, telling them the news. He had issued an official description of you at the station, but we had been told that someone would be around in the afternoon - to go through pictures with us and choose one or two that might be suitable to release to the media.

It suddenly came to me that we should take a whole film of pictures of Hope, right at this moment while she was wearing the exact same outfit you had been wearing that morning when you first went missing. I grabbed the camera we had taken to the beach, what seemed like so long ago. We took pictures of her inside, outside, and most importantly - we thought - sitting in the pushchair, then lying in the pushchair - with her eyes closed, just like you had been.

Inevitably, I would be 'warned' by the police that afternoon that doing so had tampered with the evidence – the same evidence that they had told me to take home. I appreciate that everyone has failings and people make mistakes, but they were professionals in all of this and I was simply the distraught mother of a missing child. They should have known better than to aim such cheap blows at the victim's family in order to cover their own shortfalls. The apology they would issue later would never be enough.

I ran the film down to the chemist for processing in one hour, literally ran there and back without talking to anyone, other than the woman who took the film – a friend of a friend. I was desperate to escape the house for a moment but eager to get back for any kind of news.

Sitting at home that afternoon was, honestly, the worst afternoon of my whole life. Time seemed to stop. Minutes seemed like hours. Rosie's mother turned up with a pie. What is it about tragedy that makes people think you need or want pies or casseroles? I know that she meant well, but I couldn't focus on food. I didn't want to eat. I didn't want normal life to carry on without you.

Rosie offered to take your sister to the park, but we couldn't bear the thought of losing her too and of her being far away so instead, she took her up to play in the attic bedroom. Hope had barely spoken all afternoon, but then that was hardly surprising was it, given the circumstances? I didn't have the strength to deal with her needs, which I know sounds awful. In those early hours, I found it painful to look at her, since she was such a powerful real life reminder that you were gone.

Just before it was time to go and collect the photos, a uniformed police officer and a woman dressed in normal clothes came to the door. The woman, Mary, would be our Family Liaison Officer (FLO) and the police Officer had come to deliver her to us. She had been trained to deal with parents in such situations. I wondered, how do you train for such disasters? How can you relate to hideous crimes - crimes that have never happened to you? Mary brought no news. She made a pot of tea and talked to us about the things that you liked. She was calming in an odd way; as calming as a complete stranger, sitting in on one of the most private moments of our life can be, I suppose. Jack told her about the photos we had taken of your sister, and Mary, shocked that we had the pushchair sitting in the front garden, rang for forensics to come and take it away. FLO one, police nil.

While Jack went to collect the pictures, Mary and I began looking for what she called 'suitable' photos that the papers could run. The papers like nice-looking children who looked happy, so you, Grace, were lucky. You were beautiful. Of course, Mary had difficulty in telling you girls apart in our photos, so some of her choices had to be disregarded. We would never need age progression images though, Mary told us, because of Hope. I didn't want to think of ever needing an age-progressed image, because I thought that you would be back before we knew it.

I was beginning to become very anxious. You had been missing for several hours – three and a half, roughly. Your father spread out all the pictures of Hope - replicating you in the pushchair - over the kitchen table. At the beginning of the film were a few pictures of our afternoon on the beach and there was a picture of you in a pink dress looking out at the sea. You looked so small, so vulnerable. In that instant, I suddenly realised that we may never see you again and it was entirely possible you could be dead, murdered, or raped – a whole repertoire of unimaginable things. Things that you wouldn't wish even on your worst enemy. I broke down. I completely and utterly broke down.

"How could you have been so careless? What the hell were you thinking?" I shot at Jack.

"I would never have left her if I thought she was going to be taken. Alice, you have to believe me...."

Your father looked as bad as I felt. He never rose to the argument or said what we were both thinking – that if I hadn't coerced him into having the girls, this wouldn't have happened. If I had thought about my daughters more than I thought about my job, we wouldn't be having this discussion. He had told me so many times that we needed a new pushchair, but I had insisted that this one was fine and that we'd hardly be using it now that you were both getting older. Why waste money on a new one?

Mary talked to us about getting the emergency doctor up to the house to prescribe us drugs. We might need medication, she told us, if things took a few days to be resolved. It hadn't even dawned on me. The first night, she said, we wouldn't sleep and that would be fine, natural even. But if it carried on, we would have to take care of ourselves. If they find any evidence, she continued, we might find it difficult and need something to take the edge off. I didn't want to think about any evidence, let alone any 'happy' drugs. I would never be happy, until I had you back, until I could sleep at night knowing you were safe. Little did I know then, all the years of sleepless nights that would follow.

Chapter Seven

The picture of Hope sitting in the pushchair - pretending to be you just before you were taken - became one of the main pictures for the campaign. By three o'clock we had a few pictures of you that were ready for the press with a short piece of information covering the bare facts of when and where you were taken. Your father pushed for a live broadcast from our house on the six o'clock news. The police were reluctant, because it hadn't even been twelve hours yet let alone twenty-four. Children go missing *all the time*. More often than not, they turn up. There was no need to panic, yet.

Mary told us that we should expect to be briefed on progress at the station. Perranporth station was clearly more suited for petty theft and minor crimes, so it seemed that the officers were rather taken aback by this sudden unexpected event, therefore forthcoming information was slow.

By five o'clock nothing had changed. The police had no leads. There had been no sightings of anyone strange in the area, no signs of anyone running off with you or putting you into a car. A press conference was called for 8 pm, after only a snippet of information was reluctantly allowed to go live for the six o'clock news – a brief mention of your disappearance and a flicker of your picture.

We were told that our best chances of finding you were to include Hope in the conference, to have her image streamed out across the nation. They told us that we should try to keep calm, but to appeal to anyone who may have any information on anyone acting suspiciously, in or around the area, from 10am that morning.

When I watch the past footage back now, I'm surprised at how 'together' we seem. How normal we appear as we address millions of people across the UK, as if it were an everyday occurrence. Inside though is a rage of anger, and you could have cut the tension between your father and I with a knife. *"Please,"* I sob to the cameras *"if you know anything or have seen anything suspicious, report it straight to the police. We just want to know that our little girl is safe, and have her back home where she belongs."* The footage shoots to a ten second screening of a very subdued looking

Hope, playing in a back room with Rosie. It zooms in on her face. The newsreader takes a pause for a second longer than normal, before moving on to the next story.

The rest of the evening has become a blur in my memory. We were asked, again, questions about anything unusual we had seen over the last few days. Did anyone have any grudges? Did we owe anyone any money? The crucial questions were always aimed at your father. Why would you leave a two-year-old outside, alone, in broad daylight? Why didn't you replace the pushchair? What exactly was wrong with the nursery?

Sleep didn't come that night. Hope was restless and kept waking up, pointing to your empty cot. She couldn't understand your sudden disappearance and we didn't have the right comforting words to ease her pain. It was upsetting for us all. Mary made us cups of tea. My father arrived and took order of the day-to-day things that needed to be done – the shopping, the washing, watering the plants. It's funny - how the most normal, mundane, everyday jobs are a daunting task when your daughter is missing. I couldn't even bring myself to water the plants to allow them new life - when your life seemed so uncertain. Your other grandfather, Ray, held a special candlelit prayer service in his church to pray for your safe return to us. They showed footage of the church that had probably never been full for several years on the ITV news. Your grandfather quoted a section of the bible. Still, you didn't come back.

All I can really say about that time is that the minutes rolled into hours, which rolled eventually into days – slowly, as if life were running in slow motion. We answered all the questions we were asked. We had a lot of press coverage. Vast amounts of people called in with information. Leads were followed, but none of them really led anywhere.

It was an emotionally frustrating time for all of us. I became frustrated at the system. There were several sightings of an unaccountable older woman driving in and out of the village, seemingly alone. There were further sightings of a man with a blonde toddler, looking lost. Who were these people? Why hadn't they come forward? What did they have to hide?

Border control had been alerted, and passports were being checked with scrutiny. All of this was of course in the days before children needed their own passports in the UK. How easy it would be to remove a child on the passport of another child of a similar age. Names written in the back of an adult passport, without a picture of the infant. It made me feel sick to even think about it. It's not like it is now. The USA takes retina scans of babies' eyes upon entry. I was annoyed when the US passport control officer had to wake up Ethan to take a picture of his eyes, before I realised - that such a tiny act could have saved you. It's always better to be safe than sorry, isn't it?

There were more press conferences, newspaper interviews and TV appearances. Nothing came from it. I was alive, but not living. I couldn't eat or sleep. My dreams had haunting images of where you could be, of who could be hurting you - I became a wreck - reduced to relying on others and not being able to focus or think about anything, except you.

A week had gone by when the head of the local police came to the door. We had been warned by Mary that this could be coming. The search would be scaled down. They had no real idea of where you could be. They had searched the bottom of rivers, the coastline and the neighbouring villages. They were unsure if you should be classed as 'presumed dead' or 'abducted'. In such a prolific case, without you being returned to us, they simply didn't know what to think or what more to do. They ran the scaled down search for another fortnight. Investigators continued to man phones and filter through new evidence.

Hope kept us going. I shudder when I think back to those days now, even ten years later. The pain and the anguish of losing you was unbearable. We had to keep going for Hope. We had to believe that you were being looked after and loved. There was no other option. Without Hope, I could have easily withered and died. I thought about all the parents I had seen on the news over the years, the parents of other missing children. The parents whose only child had been taken - how did they go on?

The most difficult point in those first few days and weeks happened a fortnight later on April 29th. We were told by Mary that the body of a small child had been washed up near Plymouth. The corpse had been badly battered by the tides. Your father had to go and identify the body. I waited with Hope and my father for the news. I was torn between two thoughts – that it couldn't be you but if it was, at least all of this would be over. All the waiting, all the uncertainty.

The body turned out to be that of a much older girl, with darker hair. Later, police in Plymouth would be reprimanded for jumping to conclusions, because there was no way that a body of that size could have belonged to a child of two-years-old. Unnecessary to put us through more pain.

I desperately clung to your father when he returned, like a baby orangutan would cling to its mother. We cried tears of happiness that you were still out there somewhere and tears of sadness for the family of the unknown girl who was now lying dead with no one to mourn her.

From that moment, we decided we would carry on searching for you regardless. We could not afford to think for even half a second that we wouldn't find you or that you were being mistreated in any way, shape, or form. Good parents would never give up on their child. Good parents would do whatever it took to get you back.

Chapter Eight

Our lives continued without you, as the scaled-down search continued. Your father took some compassionate leave from work. I spent my days with Hope who had become withdrawn and clingy. The house still had a flurry of people coming and going. We worked with the police; we worked with the newspapers. We allowed strangers to come into the most painful and personal part of our lives and ask questions about how we were feeling, how we were coping. We wanted as much free publicity as we could get; we wanted you to be out there in the forefront of everyone's thoughts.

Weeks had passed by. I lost a lot of weight. It was hard to enjoy life, when I knew you were out there, needing to be found. I took Hope to the park to play on the swings. A tabloid later published a picture of us smiling and a column, *'Grace is still missing, but the Robinsons continue life'*. It was distasteful. I didn't want anything to negatively affect the search. We wanted more than anything to have you back with us, but we also had to go on, for Hope. You can understand that, Grace, can't you?

As weeks turned into months, the search continued. Investigators focused on a theory that you had been taken abroad. A girl at a sweet shop in Venice had been spotted who looked just like you. Another girl in Australia had been photographed on a beach by a British couple who were travelling. All false trails.

Public interest was huge. Support from strangers overwhelmed us. We received vast amounts of money from the very first day you were gone. There was a *'Finding Grace'* fund on top of the reward for her safe return. It soon grew into the thousands, hundreds of thousands, even. With us both out of work, it occurred to me that we didn't have the financial means to able justice to be sought. How much money would it take? It eased the pressure, knowing that we could focus on finding you, without having to worry about how we would afford the bills or put food on the table.

The daunting obstacles and legislation around missing children was a complete minefield. We hired our own private investigator, Edward Harper, who seemed much more thorough than the local police. He wanted lists of all children who had left the UK the month after you had gone. Computer systems then were not as they are now, so this became a long and drawn-out job. Getting information from different government departments was a difficult process. Getting the police to share what they knew was even worse.

Life began to have a new pattern. Every day we heard from our private investigator Edd; every few days the police briefed us on their progress, or lack of it. We wrote out pages and pages of people who we knew, people who may have a grudge against us and people we were related to. In eighty percent of child abduction cases the abductor is known to the family. Every person we had ever known became significant. No stone would remain unturned.

Local police were becoming less helpful as time went on. The local people were becoming tired of a police presence in the village. Holiday season was nearly among us and tourists would flock. They didn't want to see police looking for bodies along the coastline. They didn't want them to think that it could happen to them, that their child was at risk. They wanted to enjoy the weather and the sea without worrying that their child could be taken in a split second.

Posters went up all over the village about staying safe, about keeping children close. They employed extra lifeguards that summer to keep a more watchful eye over those extra children swimming, and playing on the beach. Just to be safe, they said.

Your father kept himself busy with Edd, the private investigator. He spent his time calling in favours from people who he knew who had access to files, finding out if sex offenders lived nearby, if our neighbours were people with tainted pasts – the people we went to coffee mornings with, the people we said hello to every morning when we went out for the morning papers.

Megan's Law was live in the USA, but we, in so-called 'Great' Britain were simply miles behind. We didn't worry about things like that - then. When you are the victim of a crime, you start to see everyone under a suspicious light. You question everyone's motives. You wonder - why the UK didn't seem interested in protecting its children.

That first summer you were gone, Grace, I found it difficult to carry on. Later I learned that this is a normal part of the grieving process for someone who has lost a child. I could barely leave the house for fear of being recognised, for fear of being approached by strangers. It became particularly difficult to do things with Hope. The whole country had been flooded with images, so it was a natural reaction for people to stop and look, to make sure that Hope was herself and not you. Several people phoned the police with sightings of Hope with unfamiliar people. Rosie had taken to only taking her out when her mum was around to oversee, after being accosted by some well-meaning tourists.

Missing people became my focus. I began to research all the people who had gone missing over the years. I thought one of the cases might highlight a clue, might make me see things from a different point of viewpoint. Some of the cases were hard to read - many of the children ended up murdered or raped. A little boy was murdered in America sixteen years before you were taken. His story was turned into a TV film and the end of each broadcast showed pictures of missing children all over the USA. Because of the footage, many children were found and returned home, including Bizzy Bone a now famous American rapper.

I was beginning to learn that so many children disappear into thin air. So many are taken from supermarkets, garages, and hotel rooms. Some of them simply never return home from school. Many are taken from people with money and power and are held for large ransoms. Yet, some of them do return and are found well many years later. It's these cases that yield hope for the parents who are still looking, for people like us.

Summer came and went with no real leads, with no new information on where you had gone. September was a difficult month, as your third birthday approached. I was beginning to realise that Hope needed some real help. Like all of us, she had lost the person she once was and had become a shadow of her former, happier-self. We bought two gifts – two wooden farm sets with little matching animals. We wrapped them and wrote two matching cards. Your father put your gift in your half of the room that you shared with Hope.

There was no party. There was no cake. There were no squeals of laughter or delight from our two beautiful daughters. We were left with half of a whole and we felt it - badly. It had been nearly six months without you. The work needed to bring you back had only just begun.

Chapter Nine

I began taking Hope out to do things that I used to do with you both – outings to the park, and picnics on the beach. The first few times were really quite strange. I wore big sunglasses and put a large hat on Hope that covered most of her face. Most people had lost interest in us, besides that general feeling of *'isn't it awful?'* They held their children for a second longer. At night, they might tell them they love them, watch them sleep and be glad it didn't happen to them. We were left to carry on as we once had.

Jane came over a few times with Poppy and it was nice to talk about things that didn't matter – who had been for a haircut, where people were going to send their children to nursery. I enrolled Hope at the local school and she did five afternoons a week after Christmas. Occasionally, Jane offered to take Hope and Poppy to the park for an hour. "You need a break," she said, eyeing me suspiciously. She was right. I had become too clingy with Hope; too unsure of who she was safe with. Part of me wondered if whoever had taken you, Grace, would come back for your sister. Yet, another part of me wanted to believe that what had happened to you kept her safe – that I had to be the unluckiest person on earth if I had two of my daughters stolen from me.

Edd was working flat out, following leads and providing us with more information. Your father called and visited people all over the country. We became distant as we followed different avenues in our search for you. He slept in hotel rooms all over the place and often forgot to call. Though we always tried to show a united front for those all-important TV interviews, the seams of our relationship were beginning to collapse. He blamed himself for what had happened. I found it difficult to reassure him, because he was the one who left you alone. Although I blamed myself in many different ways, the blame itself became a silence between us, which only heightened our distraught relationship. Looking back now, I could have done more. I should have pointed him towards professional help at the very least. I think the truth was that I was so wrapped up in my own pain that I couldn't focus on anyone else's. It's another poor excuse, I know.

Christmas became the next event in our lives that crept up on us. Big events were always the hardest to handle. I'd like to say, that over all these years' things became easier, but that isn't the case. Even now, you have a place at our table. You have become the literal "missing piece."

I spent that Christmas with Jack's parents, your grandparents, and Hope. Your father was *'too busy'* to join us. Although it was a traditional family Christmas, they had scaled it down and refused other visitors. We did what we could to not upset each other. We kept our thoughts about you to ourselves.

Returning to Shell cottage after the holiday was hard. I became aware of all the things that belonged to you that remained in the house. Clothes that you would never wear again, because you already would have outgrown them, like your sister. I took them to a local homeless shelter, without telling them who I was or why I had bags full of unworn clothes, many with labels intact, many bearing expensive designer labels. The pain on my face probably said it all, as I placed the bags on the counter and left. What else could I have done with them? I felt uneasy giving them to anyone I knew. Surely, it would have been bad luck of some kind.

Hope had been sleeping in my bed with me for some months now. She had never settled back into that old room without you. Her drawers full of clothes had already been moved into the spare room. I got the joiner back and told him to take down the staircase. He told me he would keep it stored because I would probably want it back one day. I bit my tongue. What is a wooden staircase compared to a daughter?

February and March disappeared. We were approaching the one-year anniversary of your disappearance and it was a sad, dark time for us all. Jack became more and more withdrawn. He had refused to come with me to some interviews on breakfast television. I was worn out from all the travelling to and from various TV studios, radio stations, newspaper offices. I couldn't turn down the offer of any free publicity, anything to keep your name and picture up there. Anything that *might* bring you back.

We decided that we would go to the top of the local cliffs in Perranporth and release 365 balloons, which were made with a single word of text - 'Grace'. Each balloon represented every day you had been gone. The press came to film the event, and people had travelled from both near and far. Jack and I wanted each balloon to go to a person who had known our daughters, our families and friends. People who sacrificed parts of their own lives while they were out looking for you, for nothing other than consideration towards our family.

Your father stood next to me - as we counted down from ten to let all the balloons go. The camera crew focused on Hope letting go of her balloon and then panned out to the sky where the hundreds of pink balloons rose upwards. People stood with tears running down their faces in silence for several minutes after.

Jack began to speak;

"It has been one year to the day that we last saw our little girl, Grace. We never dreamt one year ago that we would be standing here without her. We never thought for a moment that we could live our lives without knowing if she was safe. Every day we love and miss her more. We will always believe that she is out there waiting to be found. Thank you, to all the people who have looked for her, and thank you, to all the people who will carry on looking - regardless of red tape, regardless of other duties they may have..."

People nodded in agreement as your father finished his speech, the speech that would be his last.

Less than two hours later, he was found in the local woods hanging from a tree. He had written one word in sticks beneath him, *'Sorry'*.

*

Human compassion can be a wonderful thing. Without it, I couldn't have managed those first few days without your father. We had drifted apart, but I hadn't imagined that he was so low, that taking his own life would be an option worth anything more than a passing thought in those dark times. Now, there was nothing I could do to bring him back or make him realise that bad things happen to good people for no reason.

It was hard to imagine that one year ago we were a happy family of four. Now, there were only two of us left. I should say that there were two of us left and one unaccounted for. I felt overwhelmed with grief, I felt alone, and I felt angry with your father for taking the easy way out. I was left to carry on searching for you and to care for the one daughter I had left. How would I manage?

We buried Jack a few days later in the local church. The sun shone and the birds sang. Hundreds of people filled the church. They had to turn some people away. I don't know, to this day, who they all were, because we certainly didn't know that many people.

Your grandparents wanted your father cremated, so we scattered his ashes out to sea later on that week - just us, they way it should be. Afterwards, we went out to Jack's favourite tearoom and sat drinking tea and talking about the good times through our tears and pain.

Consumed with my own grief, I felt for Ray and Joyce as they said goodbye to their son. Jack was a good man. A man who made a mistake that he paid for with his own life. He lost one daughter and now he wouldn't see the other one grow. He would miss Hope's first day of school, her parents' evenings, her exams. She would never be able to talk to him about things that mattered to her.

Joyce stayed with us for some months after Jack had gone. I think she wanted a new purpose in life; she wanted to feel that she could make up for your father not being around. I enjoyed her company. I enjoyed talking to her about Jack as a boy. I enjoyed sharing Hope, the little things she did at nursery that seemed unimportant to anyone else but us.

Someone said to me once, that you should never regret anything that leads to your children. Once, Jack and I had something special. He gave me two beautiful daughters. He became a man I didn't know when he slipped away from us. But he will always have a place in our hearts as we go forwards on our journey. No matter where we end up, he will always be a part of our story, a part of us.

I'm not sure what else I can tell you about this time, Grace. I will tell you though, that one thing I learnt is this: you never know how strong you are - until being strong is the only choice you have.

Chapter Ten

Although life changed for me dramatically, I remained focused on doing what I could to get you back. After your father was gone, your grandmother moved into the spare room and she took over the day-to-day tasks of cooking and cleaning. I suppose that she wanted to help, and I wanted – needed - someone to be around. It suited us all.

Hope became more and more withdrawn. Social services came to the house to complete a report on her well-being. It seemed a little silly to me. She had lost two of the people she loved the most in one year; she was bound to be unsettled and more nervous in life than she had been before.

The social worker seemed to be one of those new types, the ones who think that any problem can be fixed quickly if you do the right things. She brought Hope some picture books; *'Badger's Parting Gifts'* was one of them. I didn't mind her trying to help, but I didn't like her putting you, Grace, being missing under the same umbrella as Jack. Your father was gone, but you would come back to us. I did not want Hope to have any doubts about it. I did not want her to be told that we didn't really know if you would ever come back to us.

Mary popped by at the house from time to time. We had become friends of sorts. She understood our pain and didn't make any fleeting generalisations about us.

There was very little communication from the police. As the investigation led to dead-ends, the search was simply more and more scaled back. I suspected that the police were now doing the bare minimum they needed to do in terms of trying to find you, Grace. There wasn't a lot I could do about it; I didn't have the energy to fight them. I wanted to focus any energy I had on positive things.

Edd continued to work flat out off his own back, but many of his leads had also come to dead-ends. It was like looking for a needle in a haystack. You were out there somewhere, but finding you became a long and frustrating process.

The social worker recommended that Hope saw a psychologist, one that specialised in children who have experienced death and trauma. Hope would be starting school full time in another year, which would be a big change for her, a change that I wasn't sure she would be ready for in her current state. I wanted her to be normal, to enjoy life. I wanted the social worker to cut us some slack.

In the end, I went to a private psychological firm in Newquay. I wanted the best for Hope; it didn't matter about the cost. I didn't want to wait months for an NHS advisor to become available. I didn't want to sit in hospitals - with other people to talk about the problems our children may or may not have. I didn't want to make small talk with strangers about you, Grace. I wanted anonymity. I wanted to do things my own way.

The woman who agreed to take on Hope, with all her problems, was older than me. Ten years or so, at a guess. She had a soft face and kind eyes. The eyes seemed important to me. Small children can be so nervous with strangers – untrusting of anything unfamiliar. I wanted Hope to feel comfortable and secure in what would be a strange environment for her. I felt it was important for her recovery.

The firm consisted of the female child specialist, who I learned was called Sarah, and her male work partner, Tom. She specialised in the children while he focused on the adults. When I went to the office alone to talk to Sarah about Hope, about how much support she might need - I was struck by the friendliness of a place that could easily be sad. A bright waiting area held a coffee machine and the two desks of the consultants at the other side. They wanted to seem approachable, she said. There was a part-time receptionist, but they liked to operate the desks themselves when they could. They left their desks only to enter the two private rooms, a room for each, with their patients. Sarah asked for two initial 'getting to know you' appointments to find out about Hope, to try to discover how deep her feelings of loss may be. Eventually, the time came for me to take her in for a session on her own.

I took Hope in the car for her 10 am appointment. She nodded her head as I explained as best as I could that she was going to 'play' with a nice lady who worked with children who were feeling sad. They fussed over her new red shoes as we entered the building. I didn't tell them that we had to buy two pairs in the shop. That Hope had simply refused to entertain the idea of new shoes if we were not buying any for you, Grace. Another minor quirk she had developed that made our day-to-day life difficult. I made a note to put it in the diary that she would take with her to every session.

As I sat in the waiting area, I looked out the window. I brought a book out of habit, which seemed the right thing to do, but I hadn't managed to read in a long time. The adult psychologist, Tom, was sitting at his desk. He seemed to be typing up some reports on his computer. At ten-thirty, he announced he was going to get some coffee from the bakery across the street. My eyes gestured to the machine. 'Rubbish coffee! She thought it would make the place more homely for visitors, but we still both go to Frank's, twice a day,' he said. Off he went in search of two cappuccinos, and returned not long after. I smiled, thanks, as he placed mine on the table in front of me.

Hope's initial sessions went well. Her councillor was confident that she was struggling with issues of sibling separation anxiety disorder. Her case was more difficult because her brain found it difficult to distinguish her feelings between you, Grace, and her father, who would never return. It was common enough, she told me. It wasn't a classic case but she thought some cognitive behavioural therapy with some minor adjustments would make a real difference. Given the media attention we got for you, Grace, we decided the visits to the centre would be confidential. I didn't want to be faced with the press all the time. I didn't want to justify my actions to other people. I didn't want Hope to be in the spotlight any more than was necessary.

We travelled back and forth to the appointments twice a week. I quite enjoyed having something I needed to do, something that I could focus on – an excuse to leave the house. Joyce noticed what a difference it was making for Hope. I had to agree that some of her sparkle had come back after only a few sessions. The social worker had been right to push me to find her help. Hope wasn't completely back to normal; but would she ever be? How do you ever get over such a devastating loss when you aren't even old enough to comprehend it?

I began to form a friendship with Tom. Every session he brought us back coffee from Frank's. Every week our conversations would grow. He didn't treat me as if I was broken and lost. He didn't look at me with sadness in his eyes, as so many people did back then. A couple of times, I went over to Frank's with him. We sat inside, blending in with the crowd, talking about what was on TV, what our plans were for the weekend. To anyone else, we were just two ordinary people, enjoying friendship over coffee.

Hope's sessions were going to drop to one a fortnight, because of her steady progress, and I realised I was relying on my friendship with Tom more than I first thought. I joked that I would have to book myself in for some sessions with him. I gave him the phone number to the house and he called to make sure Hope and I were okay, that we were managing. I called him late in the night, the time when everyone but me could sleep, - the time when nothing good was on television. We talked about nothing in particular, just the weather, and how busy he was at work.

Your father, Grace, had been gone for less than a year. I admit that there was an element of guilt in being able to form such an easy relationship with another man so soon. Should I have stayed stuck in the past? Your father was gone. There was nothing I could do to bring him back. I felt vulnerable on my own. I needed company. I needed to move on. You can understand that, can't you, Grace?

Although Tom was nearly ten years my senior, he had no children of his own. He had separated amicably from his wife some years before we met. They wanted different things, he said. His wife had sold everything on a whim, moved to Australia, married, and had three children. It's funny how people can do that, isn't it?

Tom enjoyed Hope, made a fuss of her in the right ways, but left her to be as independent as she could be, didn't crowd her, didn't try to replace what she had lost. He came over after work some evenings for supper. On the weekends, we took Hope out, the three of us, our new little family.

Joyce decided it was time for her to move back north to be with your grandfather. I think she felt a bit in the way, as if her purpose had been achieved. She didn't seem angry at me for moving on so quickly. *'It's what Jack would have wanted,'* she said. *'You can't live in the past'*. Still, I was sad to see her go. I made her promise to come back whenever she wanted. I told her it didn't matter what happened to me in my personal life; she would always be a grandma to Hope and would always have a place with us.

I watched Hope, as her happiness began to return. She became the girl she used to be, laughing, giggling, and chatting with her friends. She strove for the company of girls her own age, and we didn't know it then, but that was one of the little things she never really shook – being able to manage on her own. I always looked at her and thought of you, Grace. We – Tom and I - always talked about how you would enjoy the moment too.

Tom asked us to move in with him. He had a house just outside of Newquay, and we would be more anonymous there, a bit more out of the way. His house had a large garden, and you could walk down to the sea that we could see from the kitchen window. The neighbours were elderly and didn't concern themselves with gossip. We chatted with them over the fence that separated the two gardens. They didn't ask prying questions, but we knew they cared in their own way. Tom had a black Labrador called Ben who Hope loved. She chased him all around the garden, throwing balls and sticks. We would be safe living at Tom's. It seemed practical and logical. You can't be alone forever.

Jack's London apartment needed to be sold, so I worked on making that happen. I didn't have the time or energy to organise two house lets, and I wanted to move on. Rosie, who was now studying for her childcare qualification, moved into the apartment, and the house was rented out to holidaymakers. We would return to the house one day, but for now it was time to let it go.

The money was split between you girls and put into your savings accounts. There wasn't as much money as there could have been, because there was still a mortgage to pay, and suicide meant that your father's life insurance wasn't valid. I could see their point, but who, really, would take their own life for money? I dealt with things as best as I could.

We needed to be free of the place where so many bad memories lingered. We needed a new house - for new memories to be born. You will always have a place with us, Grace; no matter what changes occur in our family. Every house we lived in had a room for you, ready for when you come back. You had a new life now, with a new set of parents - a life without us. We needed a new life too. We needed a fresh start so that when you came back to us we could make it right.

Chapter Eleven

The next two years in our house outside Newquay remained mostly uneventful. We kept pictures of Hope in the limelight as much as we could without causing her too much stress and anxiety, without dragging her to a different TV studio every day of the week. She needed to live her own life without being constantly reminded that you were missing.

I walked Ben down to the beach on most mornings. I chatted with the other dog walkers about idle things. I wondered if some of them really knew who I was, or if they were just being polite by not mentioning your disappearance, Grace.

We still had Edd working for us in his search to find you. He had been all over the county visiting people who he thought might have a link with you, anyone who seemed suspicious. He called every few days or so. It was lucky that we could still afford to pay him out of the fund. We decided some time ago to move him on to a salary pay instead of him billing us for the hours he did. It worked well for us because it meant we would pay Edd a little less, which would free up money for other things, like publicity. All Edd really wanted was to be able to pay his bills, and to have a bit extra. You don't get a lot of human compassion these days. There is always someone looking out for themselves first, wondering what they can get out of something. Edd often joked that when you were back we would have to build him an apartment over the garage so that he could carry on looking for other missing children, without worrying about paying the rent.

It was a funny time because computers were really starting to take off. A trial of the Missing Children website went live in 1998. It would take years for it to be what it is today, but it was a big step in the right direction. A lot of the old paper records were being updated to electronic versions. Edd managed to access copies of every child leaving the UK from the day you were taken to a month afterwards. It took him some time and I didn't dare to ask him how he eventually came across them. Luckily, not as many people went abroad with young children back then. The list, though, still ran into the thousands. If he spent only one day following up each child – well, you can see that it would take him years and years to work through his list.

In 1999, Tom and I became engaged. It seemed the right thing to do for everyone. It would make our lives more solid, make us harder to break. We would become the Smith family. We laughed a little at the irony of it – I would go from being one of the most recognisable mothers in the country to a Smith; I'd blend in with any crowd. I could reserve a table for dinner without people giving me a table out of pity. I could go back to having a quiet life, at least for some of the time.

Hope was five when we married. She wore a little cream bridesmaid dress with roses embroidered down one side. I wore a simple summer dress, plain but classy. We didn't want a big wedding that would draw attention to us. We decided that we would only have very close family and a couple of friends. That's what happens, isn't it, when you have been married before? Particularly when my first marriage breaking down was based on such tragic circumstances. You can't have a really happy day, with the rest of your life ahead of you, when all you really want is the one thing that is missing. That's been the hardest bit, you know, Grace. Finding a balance.

After the wedding, we decided we moved north to Wales. Tom became the partner of his own practice, which allowed him to have more family time – by being his own boss. We found a lovely house just outside Beaumaris on the Isle of Anglesey. It had five bedrooms and the sea wasn't too far. It seemed important for Hope to be in a place that wasn't too dissimilar to what she was used to.

The local school was good. There, she would just be one of a whole class. She'd never feel as if everyone were talking about her, wondering if her sister would come back. She was in a good place mentally and we wanted to do what we could to minimise anything that could unsettle her.

I decided we would start to scale back our TV appearances a little. I dyed my hair brown and had it stripped back to its normal colour when I knew that an interview was looming – an anniversary of you going missing or your birthday.

Tom wanted us to try for a baby. I was quite reluctant. I felt that you couldn't just replace what has been taken with a newer model. I didn't want the world to think we didn't care about you anymore, that we didn't love you. I didn't want the word to think we had given up on you.

Tom was a very good father to Hope. Although he may not have been her biological father, he did everything he could to make her feel loved and happy. I used to wind him up by saying that he loved doing all the family things, like taking Hope to Chester Zoo, visiting the aquarium, strolling along the side of the beach on a hot summer's evening with an ice cream. It felt wrong to deny him the chance of doing all those things with his own child. It felt wrong to let him be the father only when it suited me. So by the end of that year, a baby Smith was in the pipelines.

Chapter Twelve

On 2nd March 2000, your brother Ethan Thomas was born. He weighed seven pounds and nine ounces. He came to us after an easy pregnancy, followed by an easy birth. He was squashed through the birth canal rather than plucked out like you girls. He had a mop of brown hair, which was a shock for me, having spent years looking at two mops of blonde.

Hope was very taken with him. She was six-and-a-half and at the age when new babies are interesting and exciting. To her, he was a toy to be played with, rather than a hindrance and something that could impede her life. She showed him off to all her friends at school in the playground with admiration.

In Ethan's early days, I wondered a lot about your new family, Grace. Having Ethan brought back all those memories I had of my two little girls who grew into toddlers. I wondered if you had brothers or sisters, or if you were on your own? I wondered how you ended up there - if your parents had taken you, or if you had been bought to order, perhaps even offered at a reduced price because of all the media coverage we attracted? I wondered if you had friends your own age, or neighbours. I wondered how you were getting on at school, if you were a good reader and useless at maths, like Hope?

Looking back now, it's easy for me to see that I probably just had a mild bit of post-natal depression. I was in a wondering state that made me live in a mildly sad mood, as opposed to a really depressed one where you can't get out of bed. That is what real depression does – it consumes your life.

In his practice, Tom saw so many people with troubled pasts. Sometimes we talked about them over dinner, about what Tom was going to do to help them to have a more normal life. I remember the great sadness I had around the time of your disappearance. It wasn't a feeling that I was in a hurry to get back again.

It was now coming up to the fourth anniversary of your disappearance. I prepared mentally and physically for two weeks of TV interviews, for appearing on Breakfast TV, and for being interviewed by newspapers and magazines. It was always a very exhausting time. I didn't want Ethan to be televised or mentioned at all because I didn't want another child to be dragged into the limelight unnecessarily. Perhaps that sounds a little silly to you, extreme, or even a bit mad. A bit like how Michael Jackson used to put masks on his children before they were allowed outside, before they could be seen in public. As if it would really stop anyone who was desperate enough to steal a child.

In July of that year, a girl was taken by a paedophile and killed. The public was rightly outraged. The government tightened control over the sex offenders register. Another series of failings. Another life lost.

It was hard to stay positive when there was so much negativity around. You learn things about the 'safe' place in which you live that can be disturbing. For example, did you know that the UK has the highest abduction rate in Europe? That there are approximately 30,000 sex offenders registered in the UK alone and you won't really ever know who they are, where they live, or what they look like? That the government thinks there could be up to five percent of extra paedophiles who are living 'underground'. But if you're lucky enough to live in the United States of America you can find out where they live and what they look like before you even think about moving your family to a new neighbourhood. Did you know that in America, the chance of your child being recovered is 97%? Sometimes it takes years and years, but more and more of them are coming back to their rightful place. Many of them are initially disturbed, but many go on to lead completely normal lives.

The launch of the National Missing Children's website went live that year, 2000. It would bring many children back home and would become an important tool for missing children on an international scale.

It was a difficult year for us as a family. People wanted to talk to us about what we thought about murderers and the sex offenders' registers. They wanted to know what we thought the government *should* be doing for missing children.

You can go round in everlasting circles blaming other people, but my own guilt will always be there. It will always remain in the forefront of my mind. It will never leave me.

*

Ethan grew into a happy little toddler. He looked more like Tom than me and I was quietly grateful. I didn't want him to stand out too much, didn't want him drawing any further attention to himself. He doted on Hope. He loved Ben, the dog. We spent our days painting, drawing, and walking down to the beach, collecting shells and looking for crabs. I enrolled him in the nursery for two days to give him a little bit of independence and to make new friends. Hope settled well at school. She came out with various tales of woe most days, about which child had done what - and who had interrupted the school assembly. Tom was busy enough with work but would be home by five most evenings and only did a half day on Fridays so that we could collect Hope from school and go off and do our own things together. We had a new routine now, a new pattern.

I thought about returning to work part-time when an old colleague called me to discuss a job that had come up at Welsh Mountain Zoo in Colwyn Bay. It was a small zoo that had quite a large collection of rare animals. The current penguin keeper was leaving and they wanted someone to come in and redesign the habitat. They were also in talks at the time with other zoos on acquiring some sea lions. The zoo owners thought my previous work with dolphins would stand me in good stead to oversee this transition.

I went for an informal interview and was offered the job. I travelled in the car three times a week and Ethan would do an extra day at the nursery. I was ready for something of my own. I wanted you, Grace, to come back to a good, steady life after such an unsteady start.

Chapter Thirteen

The next few years seemed to pass us all by. We were, I think, as happy as we could be, given the circumstances. I counted all the events you were missing from: your seventh, eighth, ninth, tenth, and eleventh birthdays. The passing years didn't make it easier, didn't make our pain go away, didn't make us love you less.

Wales was the right choice for us all as a family, as the Smiths. We became friends with our neighbours, and were involved in the local community. Sometimes I laughed at what I had become, how I had managed to move on and create a new life. I found myself stood all afternoon making cakes for the school fundraiser, as if my missing daughter wasn't still out there somewhere, waiting to be found.

Hope formed some strong friendships with several girls her own age. She coped well with the transition to secondary school, as if it were an unimportant part of her life and we were all fussing over nothing. As she became older, I reminded myself that keeping her where I could see her was not good for her. She needed to be free to walk to the shops with her friends, needed independence if she had any chance of living a normal life. Ethan was five-and-a-half and was in school full-time, enjoying the social aspect more than the actual education. We talked to Ethan about you frequently, but he was at an age where he couldn't really understand, and his questions didn't have answers, which he found frustrating. We didn't want him to think you weren't there, but we didn't want to upset him either. He understood more as he grew older.

Several things changed over those years, not just for us as a family, but also for missing children everywhere. A 2003 enquiry, after the murder of two schoolchildren (by a known sex offender who managed to get a job at a primary school) resulted in thorough background checks on all adults working with children. Protecting children from such evil became imperative.

From late December 2003, in the UK, life imprisonment no longer meant life. Anyone who committed such a horrendous crime would be set a minimum term by the trial judge. The compensation offered to the victims' families was a mere £11,000.

Such a small price to pay for the life of a child. Yet it costs the government between one and fifty million pounds to give new identities to the people who assisted or withheld evidence about the murderers, who often go on to have children and live normal lives - where is the justice in that?

The missing children's website was now live and improving many children's situations. The mother of one of the children who was murdered by a paedophile released a book - talking about her experience of losing her child. The sadness, the pain. It takes a very strong woman to try to make sure that what happened to her child would never happen to another. It takes a very strong woman to challenge government policies and win.

Tom and I began to put pressure on the UK police for answers. We pushed hard for a review of the case. Edd was still working for us and he had made some quite significant leads. Most importantly, over all those years he had been working through that master list of children who left the UK around the time that you, Grace, went missing. There were now only a handful of children he hadn't traced. He needed backing from the government in order to access files that only they had the means to access. He needed them to believe that an arrest was in the pipelines, that you, Grace, would be recovered. It could only happen with police backing, police approval. Edd didn't have the legal authority to arrest, to have you removed and returned.

With the review underway, we quietly celebrated Hope's twelfth birthday with a few of her school friends. As we did every year, we put your present, Grace, in your room. You always have a room in our house. Perhaps that seems strange to you. It's always decorated the same way as Hope's so that when the time is right for you to return, everything will be ready and you will have your own space. We don't want to waste time on little things, when we have lost so much time with you already.

We worked with an agent instead of trying to handle everything ourselves. This became necessary after Jack, your father, had passed away. I used to ignore all the mail, the requests for interviews. Some of the letters were hateful. I had no doubt that some of them contributed to pushing him over the edge, in making him take that drastic step too far. All the letters were now opened by the agency. They passed on the ones that were not vindictive and bitter, that wouldn't upset us. They organised which TV shows we would appear on and what they wanted from us. Most importantly, they told us what to say to the press. I was careful with what I said about you, Grace, because I needed the press on my side at all times. They had such power in the global media.

My agent approached me with the idea of writing this book. He thought it would be good, free publicity. I wasn't that keen on the idea at first, but obviously I came round to it. The police were keen for new witnesses. Edd said it wouldn't harm our case and that getting your image and your story out there was what we needed.

We were visited by a specialist in age-progressed images. In the previous years, we simply released the most up-to-date picture of Hope. The specialist explained to me that if ill treatment was occurring, then the image we would be looking for would be drastically different. He changed Hope's face to that of a scrawny, vacant looking girl. He changed it again to a girl with darker skin, one who had been exposed to warmer temperatures. He changed it again to a fatter girl, a girl with shaggier hair, a girl who wasn't looking after herself properly. Would anyone out there recognise any of these images? We didn't really know, but we were pulling out all the stops we could.

Chapter Fourteen

It's taken me much longer to write this book than I thought. I began keen and full of enthusiasm. The reality was that I had to fit it in while looking after two children, a husband, and working three days at the zoo. I would sit late at night typing on my own with cups of coffee to keep me awake while the rest of my family slept. I poured over my memories, over the photo albums. Many of the memories were painful for me. Many of the them I chose to ignore over the years and pretended they didn't exist, because it was better for me not to think about them, better not to be haunted by strangers who may or may not have be involved in your abduction.

During this time, Hope and I talked about you a lot, Grace. About how it affected Hope over the years, about what bits of you we could still remember. Hope never complained about the things that I put her through – updating the images, the TV shows, her selfless acts over all the years. But they never brought you back.

I left some of the latter years out, but the important bits remain. Not quite thirty thousand words. I'm not really sure I can even call this a book? A novella then. Some of the best books are novellas – *'Of Mice and Men'* and *'Animal Farm'*.

Just before this book was ready to be published, just before the tenth anniversary of your disappearance, the UK published a report. A child goes missing every five minutes in the UK. One hundred and forty thousand children every year. You would think that people would be up in arms about it? But they aren't. You would think that *every single child matters,* because that's what a government manifesto wants you to believe. Most of the children have no publicity whatsoever. Some of them have no parents, no one to fight for them. Most of them aren't even on anyone's radar, because there isn't a centralised database for all the missing children. Outstanding isn't it? The nearest thing that there is to such a database estimates that there are 1418 open cases of missing children since records began. All of those parents waiting for a knock on their door that says their child has been found. All of those relatives and friends hoping and wondering for all those years.

If anyone out there has any niggling doubts about you, Grace, I employ them to please report them to the police. Maybe they knew us when we lived in Perranporth. Maybe they know someone with a little girl who seems mysterious, somehow over familiar. Maybe there is something just not right?

I often wonder if your parents, Grace, give you the world on a silver plate? Your new parents that is, assuming of course there are two of them. Assuming that there is some guilt and shame, that making you the best possible person would somehow atone for the crimes they committed in keeping you for themselves.

We all believe that this book will bring you home. That this is the final link in a series of events that will join all the dots. The new enquiry, Edd's progress, and the mass media attention we will receive on the backdrop of publishing this book. We can wait though, so you don't need to worry, Grace. We know that it is frustrating. If this isn't your time, then we gave it our best shot. We will still be here for you. We will still be waiting. You will still come home to us, one day.

One thing I have learned through all of this is that no matter how hard things are, you never give up on your children. Giving up is for the weak. Giving up is admitting failure. The only time you can justify not being there for your children, whether they are with you or not, is if you are dead. I'll keep on fighting until then. I'll be fighting for you, Grace, for you and for all missing children everywhere. We will make it right. I promise.

Part Two

Chapter Fifteen

Edd, 2006

There is always more to a person than first meets the eye. There is always something they are hiding, something they don't want you to know. Everyone has secrets.

My job is to find out people's secrets. To find the things they are trying to hide, and to recover what is lost. I've found many people over the years, people that were missing, children that were eventually returned to heartbroken parents.

Perhaps you're wondering why I am so concerned with recovering these missing people? Well, that is my own secret. As I said, everyone has a secret. If I tell you, you won't repeat it, will you? I don't want people to know, to judge me. I know they will. They always do.

When I was ten-years-old, my brother, Alan, went missing. He was walking home from school on his own one day, aged eight. He was last seen in the penny shop buying a bag of sherbet lemons. He was never seen again.

Back then, we lived on a big council estate in the Northeast of England. Newcastle. It was the sixties. The police searched the local area a bit, but that was it. They never found him, never seemed interested in bringing him back to us. There were problems with drugs and violence within our community.

My father ran off with someone else years before, left us with our mother. There was a stigma attached to single parents, back then. People pointed fingers and blamed my mother for things that were beyond her control. *No wonder she lost her boy* is what the neighbours thought along with *she probably deserved it.*

They never found Alan. Never found a single item of clothing that belonged to him. More importantly, they never found his body.

Losing Alan destroyed my mother. I had to become a man years before my time, had to be the strong one. I learned to fry eggs and cook bacon. I cleaned the house. I collected the money from the dole office, did the shopping, and paid the bills. My mother was ill, and not at all herself. She barely left the house. I made the doctors come out to her, to medicate her. They brought her back to a state of existence that was functional. I told her I would find Alan; I would find Alan and bring him home.

When I was eighteen, after working as a postman by day and in a fish and chip shop at night, I decided I was going to train with the police. I did the basic PC training, which was for two years back then. I took extra training in working with families who were distressed. I worked on cases of missing adults. I took additional courses, courses on linking evidence, on what to look out for, how to find the guilty ones.

By the time I was thirty-years-old I was retired from the police entirely. I'd made good contacts. I wanted to focus on what mattered to me - helping people trace anyone that were missing. I began to work for myself.

My mother was pleased with my choices in life. My searches for Alan didn't lead to much but at least they hadn't led to a body or to any other devastating news, which was encouraging. Mam believed he was still out there waiting for us to find him. She got older, but we still always talked about Alan. We talked about what we would say to him when we got him back, about how good it would be to have him back home with us.

I worked on cases with several missing children. More often than not, a parent had abducted them, taken them abroad. Sometimes it was hard to get them back, hard to get the other authorities to realise there had been foul play - and the child actually belonged with the other parent.

I didn't take on a case until a child was missing for some time. I learned badly, early on, that if a child was murdered evidence of it comes to light for the investigation squad in the early days. I did not want to give anyone false hope. I did not want anyone to think I was making promises that I wasn't going to keep.

I began working for Alice and Jack a month or so after Grace had first gone missing. Of course, I'd followed the story in the papers – like every other person in the country. I followed the early days, hoping for them that a body would not be recovered.

Alice and Jack were lucky in those days to have received so much media attention. The story struck a chord with me, because of Alan. Jack, in particular, made the mistake of leaving little Grace unsupervised in her pushchair outside a shop. Everyone makes mistakes, and I felt confident they would never forgive themselves for their part in what happened. How could *you?*

The case was by no means straightforward. Of course, that much is obvious, because here we are ten years later and Grace isn't home *yet*. When I began to work on a new project, I liked to focus entirely on it. I didn't take on a new case while another case was ongoing. I felt like I had to keep my head in one place at a time. There are so many strands of information, and anything overlooked could throw all my work off.

I've dabbled in and out over the years with information about Alan, but it doesn't feel disloyal to my clients. Alan is my brother, and my mother needs closure as she enters her old age. I didn't want my mother to come to the end of her own life without that closure, without ever knowing what happened to her son. I also didn't want people to think that I just gave up.

I don't mean to blow my own trumpet, but I'm close to finding Grace. It's taken me many years to reach this point. There are five children left on my list to look into. I'll visit each one personally - to make entirely sure they aren't Grace, but I am certain that one of them will be.

Once she is back home, I can put all my energy into getting all the media attention I can to find Alan. Everyone deserves the truth, no matter how difficult it may be for them to hear.

Chapter Sixteen

Richard, 2006

This is what happened when the life I knew came crashing down for the first time, five years ago...

I took my daughter to the emergency room after a bad fall in the back garden. She had jumped off the rope swing and fallen into the trashcan, slicing her head open nastily. Her mother and I were arguing in the kitchen at the time. The usual kind of arguments we had back then – I had come home from work and Kate had been drinking. The problem was beginning to spiral out of control. How could she be so thoughtless? We weren't watching our daughter at the time of the accident. She was seven-years-old.

In the hospital, while we were waiting for a nurse to come and stitch Chloe up, I bumped into an old school friend who had become a doctor in the hospital and was wandering through the children's ward. Barry. I should have made more of an effort to stay in touch with him. We had been good friends as boys – we lived in the same neighbourhood, and our parents were in the same social crowd. We remained good friends throughout college. We used to go out for a beer now and again, but it became too painful for Kate when he and his wife had three boys, so we naturally drifted apart some years before Chloe had arrived.

The hospital wanted to keep Chloe overnight for observations; they liked to be overly cautious with head traumas in children. I suppose they didn't want to end up with a lawsuit on their hands. It's better to be safe than sorry these days, isn't it?

I asked Barry to look over her chart, as a friend, as someone I trusted. I wanted to be sure that nothing was overlooked. He frowned a little as he read it, puzzled almost.

"Is everything okay?" I asked him.

"The cut is mostly superficial. It's not as deep as it looks. There isn't any permanent damage to her skull, but she's probably going to end up with a scar an inch and a half long. It will be under her hairline, so it won't be that visible," Barry said.

He paused for a long moment, wondering if he should go on.

"I'm sorry Ric, for not being there for you as a friend. I knew you had problems but I chose to ignore them."

I frowned at him. Chloe was drifting in and out of sleep in her hospital bed. I wondered what he knew? Which neighbour had told him about Kate and I having constant arguments? Which neighbour had seen her at the nine-eleven early one morning, buying more spirits, and more beers?

"Things haven't been good with Kate and me. I think we're reaching the end..."

Barry put his hand tenderly on my shoulder.

"Be careful how you play this one," he began. "It happened to a guy down the street from us. He lost all contact rights to his son through the bitter divorce. Between you and me, he said things to the Judge that should have been kept under wraps."

I wasn't sure what was happening, or what he was talking about entirely? Why would I lose all contact with my daughter? Parents get divorced all the time these days. Half the kids in Chloe's class spent their time between Mommy and Daddy, and knew no different.

"I know that it's none of my business, Ric," Barry continued, "but you never told me you used a donor. It happens to men – doesn't make you any less of a person. You would be surprised at how many people do it. But if Kate wants your life to become difficult, then this is where it's going to start."

He placed Chloe's file back in the slot at the end of the bed and started to walk away. My brain was slow to catalogue the information he had just told me.

"Hey Barry, how... how do you know that? How can you be so sure?" I asked.

He turned back to look at me.

"Do you remember when we used to give blood in college? Your blood type was A positive. Kate's blood type was A positive. The chart says that Chloe is B negative...."

His voice trailed off.

My face drained of colour. Could this really be true? The little girl I had watched come into the world, the little girl whose first words were 'Dada,' really belonged to someone else? My face must have been a remarkable sight, must have shown the disbelief I felt.

"Hey, it's ok Ric. I can't divulge this information to anyone else – its hospital policy. Just don't mention it when you're figuring out your custody arrangements, unless you only want to see your little girl through stained glass."

Chapter Seventeen

Edd, 2006

Alice's book *Finding Grace* had just hit the shelves of bookstores globally when I flew out to France to check on the first of the five children who remained on my list. I had run my usual background checks in the UK – nothing had been flagged by social services, no evidence of anything being wrong. I'd found an image of the girl at a swimming gala in a French newspaper a couple of years before. I was quietly confident that I wouldn't need long in France, that I would be looking at the wrong girl.

Alice and I had formed an odd kind of friendship over the years - a professional one that sometimes crossed over into a personal one. I was invited to the yearly release of balloons over the Perranporth cliffs - one balloon for every day that Grace had been gone. Alice became a lot more settled when she married Tom and more so when she returned to work. I found her sometimes more anxious at certain times of the year – especially the Christmases, and the birthdays. I admired the way she had managed to pick herself up and keep going. Alice was very unlike my own mother who took years to be able to function on any kind of level.

The house where this girl lived was in a nice area of town. The couple had taken the girl, when she was two-years-old, to London for a weekend on her French passport. There was no record of her being in any hospital or anywhere else during their time in London. They had moved a lot across France over the years, which is why they were more difficult to trace than other children who left the UK in the month after Grace was taken.

I parked my hire car down the street - in the French town I had arrived in and waited to get a positive glimpse of her – of the girl. I'd obtained a police warrant to question the neighbours and I'd use it if needed. I waited almost an hour before I saw the girl walk up the street with, who I assumed to be, her mother. Her hair was dark brown and wavy. The mother was white, but the girl's skin was much darker, a mixed race. This girl wasn't Grace.

*

I waited for them to be settled in the house before knocking on the door. Answered by the father, a tall coloured man, I explained in the best French I could that I was looking for a missing child the same age as his daughter and flashed a recent picture of Hope – the image of what Grace would look like today. I asked if I could just have a moment of time for a few questions and see the girl, then I would be on my way.

The family were very obliging. They were astonished they had been implicated to be of such an interest in the case for me to fly out to France. There was no question that this French girl belonged to them. They had all the paperwork, all the photos over the years. They had heard about Grace through the British media.

They wished me well with my investigation. They were sincere and genuine people. I had a feeling the others would be much more difficult, that the job would only become more difficult from here on in.

There were now four children remaining on my list. All girls. Two of them stood out the most to me. One had travelled alone from California with her mother to receive medical treatment in London. The other had travelled alone with her father, but some years later her surname was changed, and the family – the mother and a new man - moved from Spain to Austria. There were no public images for either of these girls.

I decided to go with my instinct. Austria was far closer than California; it was easier to fly around Europe than to hop on trans-Atlantic planes. The other two girls were in Vermont and New York. I didn't want to have to backtrack or make any further flights than were absolutely necessary, and I could easily head north after California. A flight to Vienna left in the morning. I called Alice to update her on my progress. I booked a seat and packed my bags.

Chapter Eighteen

Edd, 2006

The flight to Vienna took just under two hours. I picked up my hire car from the airport and headed west on the A1 towards a place called Gmuden – which took about two-and-a-half hours. It was a smallish kind of town, about 12,000 people. It had a very Austrian feel to it, though it was quite picturesque, with a lot of the town on the edge of or overlooking Lake Traunsee.

I checked into a local bed and breakfast for the evening, which was run by a very Austrian couple. I wanted to walk over to the family's last known address. I had half a hunch that they wouldn't be there since they never seemed to stay settled in any place for long – according to the records. They lived in a townhouse on the hill – mother, Stepfather, the girl, and a younger boy. Throwing caution to the wind, I knocked on the door.

Greeted by a short, stout Austrian woman, I explained in my best Austrian my reason for being there. The woman listened, eyeing me with some suspicion. She answered me in broken English;

"We be here five month. Family with girl move more west. I give address." She went inside to retrieve a piece of paper with a copy of the family's forwarding address for Salzburg. I showed her a picture of Grace, asking her if the young girl looked anything similar, if she had spoken with her at all, – if she looked distressed.

"Young girl be Austrian. Blonde hairs, blue eyes. Anna she be called. I no get good look," she responded, shrugging her shoulders.

I thanked the woman, taking the address and placing it firmly in my wallet. One slightly odd thought crossed my mind – if the family really didn't want to be found then why would they leave a stranger with a forwarding address? Why not just cut and run?

I decided I would give Alice a quick call, see if there were any big changes over there, see how the interviews were going for her and Hope. I knew that's the part she really didn't like - the constant questioning, trawling from one TV studio to another. She picked up on the second ring,

"Edd, where are you today? St. Lucia, Antarctica, the Great Australian Outback?!"

"Funny, Alice. I'm just here in Austria, soaking up some sun and hanging out with these great Austrian women...."

"Yeah, well don't forget the postcard! We've been at ITV studios today. I think it went okay. It's going live tomorrow. Hope held out well; she managed to speak for a good amount of time. The book's been flying off the shelves.... - everyone wants an interview; ABC are flying someone out here – can you believe it?!"

"Of course. Alice, your book is great. People are interested, have been interested for many years. It was always going to sell. Getting Grace's picture out there, ten years on, that's what this is about. It's all coming together now. You should be proud of yourself."

I filled her in on the events in Austria. We were both encouraged by the forwarding address, both not wanting to believe that it might lead to yet another dead end. We had come too far; we were too close to fail. I believed the answers were near, because the alternative was incomprehensible. How could we go on if all this led to nothing?

It was early evening and Salzburg was a good hour from where I was. I wandered around the main street for a while, observing the locals, taking in a new country. I decided to stop for the day, grab some dinner, and have an early night. I could be at Salzburg early in the morning if I set off straight after breakfast.

I thought of Alice's parting words as I wandered towards a row of restaurants overlooking the lake.

"It'll mean so much to all of us - when this is over. It will change all our lives; we'll be able to find peace."

I thought of Alan - on the last day I saw him alive. His smiling face, his chubby cheeks. I knew what she was saying was right, but I also knew that once we had brought those closest to us back, I'd have to keep going. So many lost people out there, and never enough people looking.

Chapter Nineteen

Edd, 2006

I got up early, breakfasted, and got the car ready for the drive to Salzburg. It was a nice day - sunny but not too warm, and the drive over was pleasant enough. The address was for a house just outside the city, down a little lane that led to a cul-de-sac of a few large, detached houses. I parked my car and had a wander around. There didn't seem to be anything unusual. I reminded myself that the family was originally from Spain, so the child may not speak Austrian or look particularly Austrian at all.

After watching the house for a while, and seeing some movement inside, I decided that knocking on the door and explaining myself would really be the only way forward. I had a gut feeling that this would be okay. So far, my gut instinct hadn't let me down.

A woman answered the door. She had a dark complexion and blue eyes. Typically Spanish looking yet blonde, and assumedly the girl's mother. I showed her my badge and told her - in my best-broken Spanish - what I was doing. She called inside the house for a man, who spoke reasonable English. They beckoned me inside.

"I am surprised you found us so easily," the man said. I wondered if I was supposed to take that as a compliment, or whether he was scolding himself for the fact he hadn't managed to keep his family well hidden.

"We, Maria and I, had trouble with Anna's father. A long dispute over custody. We took Anna from and brought her here to my country. We married and Anna has rights to be here. Spanish authorities want Anna to be back in Spain, but it is not what is good for her."

"Her father has visitation rights, but not sole custody?" I asked him.

"Yes, he is a man with money – a man with power. He beat Maria, Anna's mother, senseless time after time. Maria leaves him and finds me. We take Anna to where it is safe. We call Anna by a new name in public but sometimes she forgets and tells a neighbour her real name. Then we must move on. It is for her safety; she cannot be back in Spain with a monster."

I wondered what it were like to be these people – fugitives of the law. Running away because that's what they thought was the best for their child. I wondered how much of a monster this man really was, if he was really just a man desperate to see his child, desperate to know. Often, you hear of men keeping children from women. The children simply disappear.

The man, Frank, produced a whole pile of papers for me to look through; Anna's birth certificate, passport, change of name deeds - pictures of her from birth until now. This was not a child who had just 'appeared' to be with this family. A child they had tried to keep hidden, yes, but not for the wrong reasons.

"Grace has been missing for ten years. She has an identical twin sister. If I can just see Anna for a moment, I can leave you to get on with your life and nobody will need to know I was ever here."

Maria nodded to Frank, and then she called up the stairs to Anna.

Anna emerged down the stairs and into the living area in which we were sitting. She was a pretty girl - with blonde hair and blue eyes. She didn't look Austrian, as her old neighbour had suggested. She looked like she belonged in central Europe. Pretty though she was, she wasn't Grace. She stood for a moment, then left to go back up the stairs.

"Thank you for your time, both of you. I appreciate your honesty. Grace is out there somewhere. Hidden, maybe like Anna, but for different reasons. She belongs back home with her family."

"We hope you find the girl," Frank said. "Sometimes, a girl is better off without a father. But to take a girl from her mother, that is an unspeakable thing."

I thanked them again, and walked back to my hire car. I had a long drive back to Vienna. I stopped at an internet cafe to book my onward flight to California. I downloaded all the information Google gave me on Richard and Kate Sumner – a few newspaper articles and an address for the school Richard worked in; hardly a great deal to work with, but a start nonetheless.

I loaded my bags into the car and hit the road. The real trouble, I sensed, was about to begin.

Chapter Twenty

Richard, 2006

The second time my life came crashing down was today, some five years later. It happened to me on a day that was otherwise so *ordinary*. I was working all day, teaching math to children who were in high school.

It was late spring for us in California and the temperature was up in the sixties. Our fruit trees were bearing large, ripe fruits now; the oranges were sweet and juicy. Jen prepared us salads for supper, with hot chicken or steak. The weather was too hot for the bigger meals we had with rice or potatoes; the girls complained about them in those warmer months.

I came home from work, walked through the empty living room to the kitchen. The French doors were open to the garden. The girls, Chloe and Emily, were playing in the pool. I slipped off my shoes and sat in one of the lounge chairs.

"I'm just nipping to Wal-Mart," Jen said. "We need some pickle and Chloe needs some stuff for her school trip tomorrow. I'll pick up a cooked chicken, we are having salad for supper."

I listened to her picking her purse up off the counter and the sound of the car engine as she pulled out of the drive. Jen worked part-time as a vet. Emily was in kindergarten now, and I think Jen enjoyed being able to do something on her own, to be something other than just a Mom. The extra money came in handy too, though it dented my pride a little, as Jen earned slightly more than I did for her part-time hours.

We lived at Sunset beach in Orange County. Jen had bought the place before me, so we altered it slightly over the years to make it more child friendly, more accommodating for the girls. We were lucky to live in such a nice part of the world. Lucky for the girls to have such a laid-back approach to life.

Chloe came to us permanently some two years earlier after the state welfare officer told us that her living with her mother was no longer possible. As part of our divorce, Kate had been forced to enrol in a program to help her to sober up. It was the only way the judge was happy for her to be given the main custody rights of Chloe and for me to have a good amount of visitation. For the next two years, she attended the meetings - on and off. At one point, she looked good and the therapy seemed to be working. Just before Chloe's tenth birthday, she hit a downward spiral. Chloe came home to find her mother passed out several times; she called me, begging me to come and take care of her Mom, and not to call the authorities. '*She doesn't know what she's doing Dad,*' she would say. '*She doesn't mean to hurt us.*'

In the end, the cops picked up Kate on one of her early morning runs in the wagon for more alcohol. She was arrested for driving under the influence of alcohol. She became incapable of caring for herself, let alone a young, defenceless child. The judge issued full custody to be given to Jen and I and allowed Kate supervised visitation until she cleaned up her act.

Often, I felt bad for Chloe during those years that she was left alone with her mom. I felt bad for leaving her with a woman that was unable to provide for her child's basic needs. I paid child support. I called Chloe every day. I tried really hard to be a good father. It wasn't enough though. I wanted to fight for her, properly in court, pull out all the stops and paint Kate as a terrible mother. I was frightened of pushing Kate too far, frightened to admit to her that I knew Chloe wasn't mine - biologically at least. I could not have Kate admit this to a judge. I would never walk out on the daughter I had raised as my own.

*

Jen came home from Wal-Mart about thirty minutes later. I'd sent both of the girls upstairs to spend some time on their homework, which for Emily meant that she had licence to read some of her books and colour in unsupervised, which was still a novelty for her. Jen looked nervous, unsettled. I watched her from the garden as she fumbled around in the kitchen. I walked inside to see what was going on.

"Is everything ok?" I asked her. Her eyes glossed over.

"I saw something funny in the supermarket.... I..... Ric..... I'm not sure about this."

She handed me a bag with a hardback copy of a book. Jen was well known for picking up more books than anyone could possibly read in a weekend while in Wal-Mart. She'd taken to reading some of those true to life books, which, frankly, I found quite depressing. Who wants to read about a child who has been abused?

I picked up the book. It was by a woman whose name I didn't recognise – Alice Smith. It was titled *"Finding Grace."* Looking back at me was a picture of a paler version of my own daughter. Paler, yet identical in every other respect; the same eyes, the same grin, the way her hair fell slightly off her face – this girl was Chloe reincarnated.

My head was spinning. My mind, suddenly dizzy. My stomach churned. I put a hand out to steady myself from falling. Took some long, deep breaths. Tried to restore my body to something resembling calm. Silent tears were falling down Jen's face. How could this be? I wondered. How *could* this be?

After what seemed like an eternity of silence, Jen spoke.

"What do we do, Ric?" She asked, in a voice not much louder than a whisper.

I paused, a moment longer than I should have.

"Disconnect all the phones. Keep both girls inside. Call the school and tell them Chloe has a fever and she's going to be off sick for a few days... I will read this book cover-to-cover, overnight. We'll try to get hold of Kate. First thing tomorrow morning, we need to find a good lawyer."

Chapter Twenty One

Jen, 2006

It's funny, isn't it, the way your life can change in a moment? A simple errand with catastrophic results. I wanted to buy every book on the shelf in the store – eight blocks from where we live. I didn't want anyone we knew to see the same thing I saw when I browsed the books. *'That girl seems familiar,'* the shoppers might think, or even worse, *'Isn't that Richard's daughter?'*

Ric went to his office with the book. I went upstairs to check on the girls, both blissfully unaware of the chaos around them – Emily was playing with her wooden dollhouse and Chloe was reading her book. I wondered how we would cope if Chloe was taken from us, from the only life she had ever known – from where she belonged.

Families can be funny things; they come in all shapes and sizes. We worked hard to make a good life for our children. We were *good* parents, good people. I baked cookies for school fairs, took the girls out for ice cream on Fridays after school. I went above and beyond, trying to prove myself to other people. I wanted the neighbours to look at us and think, *'what a great job she does with those* girls' and *'Chloe is much better off with a mother like that'.* Blended families get a lot of bad press these days. I knew we were more normal than I thought, but I was proud of what we achieved as a family unit, given the circumstances.

I sometimes think back to the time before we were a real family, the time when Ric was married to someone else. Chloe would have been five. I'd started running on the beach before work and I met Ric doing the same. I was in my mid-thirties but Ric was older, in his mid-forties then. We chatted occasionally and over time, we became friends of sorts, learning little bits of information about each other's lives. Twice a week we ran together and I began to live for those mornings, when I could be with Ric and feel like a normal person.

After a while, I invited Ric back here - to this same house - to shower. It made sense. We would get ready for work, grab a bite to eat, and head out to our separate lives. I waited for Ric to decide when he wanted our relationship to go further. It seemed wrong - to prey on a man who was married with a little girl, no matter how much I knew that the marriage was all but dead. I knew that it had to be on Ric's terms. I knew it was wrong, but I couldn't help myself.

We became an unofficial couple. I never asked Ric to leave her, his wife. I knew that they were not romantically involved, that they slept in separate rooms. I was happy plodding, for now. We went through some rough times; it wasn't plain sailing. It's hard to share someone you love with other people like that. Hard to compromise.

After a couple of years, I discovered I was pregnant with Emily. I'd had an ovary removed some years before and we had discussed the problems Ric had had with his wife - trying to conceive. We overlooked contraception. I told Ric I was keeping the baby, that it didn't mean he had to leave his wife and that I didn't expect him to be here for both of us.

I wasn't anti-abortion; I just felt that it wasn't the right option for me. I could look after the baby by myself if I had to. There never is a right time anyway, is there? A baby will always take up your demands for time, for life. If the baby had managed to be there despite the odds, then that is what would happen. We would work it out and if we couldn't...then it probably wasn't meant to be for us either.

Ric struggled with it all for a couple of months – torn between his two families. Then Chloe fell and cut her head after an argument he had with Kate about her drinking problems. '*She isn't mine,*' he told me. It didn't make our problems any less, but it did give him the strength to leave his wife - of his own free will - to start a new family, a new life with us.

What followed was a simple divorce and a straightforward custody arrangement. Chloe would be with us every other weekend and two nights in the week. She loved Emily. I admired Ric for doing the right thing by her, it broke his heart when he found out what Kate had done, but you never leave your child no matter what life throws at you.

Chloe was a great kid, and it was a relief for both of us when she came here permanently. Ric said that when the time was right, when she was much older, we would help her understand about her biological father – the one that provided the goods but did little else. We talked about him as a 'non-person'. That is what you would have to be, right, if you knew you had a child out there and didn't do a damn thing about it?

On the outside, we were just a normal American family. On the outside, we were the same as everyone else. We loved both our girls - equally. We would go to have picnics on the beach on warm days, vacations to Canada, and Mexico. I don't think I will ever be entirely comfortable with Ric leaving his wife for us, but isn't that what makes us human? The ability to think about people other than ourselves? I've had to remind myself over the years that it wasn't as bad as I thought – that it wasn't as if he was in a happy, loving relationship with someone else. Somehow, that makes it feel a little better. Eases my conscience, even if it's just a little.

I wondered - how we would manage this - if it really was true? That Kate took her, Chloe, and brought her up as her own? That's what the blurb on the book was suggesting. I'd flicked through the first page or so in the car and hadn't dared to read anymore. This girl was taken when she was two-and-a-half – a toddler; a talking, walking, little girl. Was Ric really an innocent bystander? How can you not notice that your daughter isn't the same anymore?

I've always kept Kate at a distance over the years. I can't say that I hold any personal grudges over the woman. More so, she probably harbours ill feelings towards me for taking what was hers and claiming it for myself - or more correctly, for my own family. We spoke in passing when it was necessary – school plays, parents evenings, that kind of thing. There was something about her I always found a little odd - her protectiveness over Chloe; her inability to communicate with us.

This time, though, she owed us the truth. We needed her to make sense of all of this. We needed her to tell us that this is all a big mistake. That the girl we loved as our daughter had not been stolen. That our family would not be broken apart. I picked up the phone, and I dialled her number.

Chapter Twenty Two

Richard, 2006

I locked myself in the office. Locked. I never locked the doors to any rooms, but today it felt necessary. I couldn't risk Chloe walking in to see me reading a copy of a book with her picture sprawled across the front. I couldn't risk Jen coming in here, asking me questions. Watching, wondering.

I couldn't read the book. I stared at it for a long time before deciding to Google this missing girl - Grace Robinson. How wonderful the internet can be. How ironic that the information was at the tip of my fingertips. I found enough articles to patch together what had happened to the girl. She was taken from a pushchair outside a village shop in Cornwall in England ten years ago.

Chloe was just a toddler back then. I thought back to that time in our lives, where we had been and what we were doing. She wasn't born perfect. All those years, all those years of trying to conceive, all those failures. I was ready to give up when Kate discovered she was pregnant *again*. We didn't even talk about the baby until fourteen weeks. They picked it up on a twenty-week scan – and saw the abnormality with her heart. Too late by then though, because Kate had made it to twenty weeks, which she had never done before and was a miracle in itself. She wasn't going to let anyone take her baby away now.

When the new baby, Chloe, arrived she was perfect. From the first day I saw her, she was a real daddy's girl. She slept in our room. We bought a special mattress that made noises if she was breathing irregularly. She *seemed* perfect. She was, of course, to us, but she wasn't really. She was smaller than the other children were. Taking care of her required a little extra effort. By one-year-old, she was a sickly little girl. The paediatrician sent her for more tests. Her perfect little heart was deteriorating, wasting away - Cardiomyopathy, they called it.

For the first year, we went together to every appointment, every scan. I took time off work on a regular basis. Chloe had a minor operation. After that, real life – including work - had to carry on. The headmaster at my school could only be sympathetic for so long before I had two choices – stay and stop taking the time off, or leave. Someone had to work to pay the bills; someone had to cover the mortgage. It went without saying that 'someone' was me. So Kate started taking care of Chloe on her own.

By her second birthday, Chloe was very sick. She was permanently in the hospital, needing oxygen, and needing help to function on a basic level. Kate was British. She wanted to take Chloe to London for what she called 'the best' treatment that was available – in the land where it didn't matter what your insurance did or did not cover. I could hardly say no, could I? If something bad happened to Chloe, I'd never forgive myself. It was the beginning of our marriage going downhill. I wanted Kate to stay here, to try and work things out together. However, I also didn't want to lose my ailing daughter in the process. So I let her go.

Kate took Chloe to London. Almost immediately, she ended up being admitted into a children's hospital just north of London. I had a conference call with the children's heart specialist. There was a good chance that Chloe would be okay, there was an operation they could perform that would bide her time, let her get bigger and stronger. It was the only thing that would save her. That operation was a called a heart transplant.

The transplant took place sooner than expected because of the severity of Chloe's condition and the fact that a recipient donor had become available. It went well. They kept Chloe in the hospital for a month or so. The anti-rejection drugs were working. There were no ill effects, nothing untoward going on, nothing to be concerned about.

Kate flew back to California after a couple of months, but took Chloe to stay with a friend in San Diego for another couple of months after that, and then took her to my parents in Colorado for an extended break. Kate kept making excuses. I wondered if the time on her own had made her realise that she didn't want to be married anymore, that didn't want to come back to her husband. By the time Chloe came home, I hadn't seen her in almost a year.

It was after that that things really got difficult between Kate and I. The drinking began, and the paranoia about keeping Chloe safe seemed to escalate. She was overprotective and I shrugged it off – a good mom would be overprotective if her child had nearly been lost. *Nearly.* Kate had taken her for her routine appointments at the local hospital and there was nothing to worry about. After a while she was discharged from the regular outpatient's appointments. The doctors told Kate that she could '*lead her life as normally as any other child her age.*' If only it were that simple.

I thought back to the time when Barry told me that Chloe wasn't mine, biologically. It hadn't occurred to me, hadn't even crossed my mind that she didn't belong to Kate either. I was there when she was born, watched her emerge. I wondered, how Kate had managed to end up with someone else's child? What *had* she done? Where was the real Chloe? Where was our daughter?

I tried calling Kate, but it kept going to her voicemail. Typical that the one time we actually needed to speak with her she was busy, no doubt chatting idly to one of her friends about nothing important. I wondered if she had any idea about the publication of this book, any idea that this was going to happen?

My mind focused on Chloe, sitting upstairs in her room without the faintest idea about any of this. It must be a mistake, surely? For ten years, she'd been missing. Ten years that she'd been with us. Would they come here and take her away from us? Expect us to willingly hand her over? Say, '*Sorry, we have your daughter, but you can have her back now.*' Would they expect Chloe to give up all of this, give up her family to live with strangers? Do we walk her down to a police station and hand her in, knowing what we know? Or do we sit it out until someone realises who she really is, until the police come knocking on our door? What really is the best thing for Chloe?

It was getting late now, Emily would be asleep. I didn't leave the office to say goodnight to the girls, I left Jen to deal with all the practicalities – baths and story time. United we stand and divided we fall. We can do this; we can keep the family together. I had to believe it. I called my lawyer and asked her to come round first thing in the morning. I stressed the emergency of the situation. I put the book in the safe and locked it. I left my office and went back to my family.

Chapter Twenty Three

Edd, 2006

The drive to the airport went relatively easily. I checked in my bag, grabbed a quick coffee, and boarded the first plane to Amsterdam. The trouble with Eastern Europe was you're out on a limb a bit – you have to fly through central Europe to get to the other side of the Atlantic or Pacific with one of the trans-Atlantic carriers. Amsterdam airport was quiet; I had a couple of hours to have a walk around and stretch my legs. It was a fourteen-hour flight in total, but the time difference meant I'd land in Los Angeles at just after three o'clock, Pacific Time.

I didn't mind the long flights. It gave me a chance to relax a little, watch a film, and eat the countless amounts of food they bring you to distract you from your journey. You can chat with strangers to fill in the time. A woman who was sitting behind me was reading Alice's book. I was glad to see it being taken across the Atlantic, though I knew that the USA had imported thousands of copies for a reduced rate to be sold at Wal-Mart. Whoever thought of putting books in a supermarket must be laughing now – all those women popping in for the weekly shop can easily sneak in a book that's only a few pounds. With the rising cost of food shopping, most people wouldn't even notice the increased cost of a couple of paperbacks.

LAX was a busy airport. I collected my bags and walked round to the car hire place, which was just outside the building. I hired a modestly small car by American standards, but was handed the keys to what I would have called a large four-door family estate in the UK. Complete with those all-American features – automatic drive, cruise control, air conditioning. The man in the hire centre threw in a sat-nav with the car, which was handier than having to buy a map and check it every five minutes - geography never had been my strong point. The car was full of petrol and I was surprised at how cheap it was over here. No wonder people didn't walk more than a couple of blocks.

I rented a room at a hotel in Seal Beach. It was around a half-hours drive from the airport, but close enough to the house that Richard shared with his new wife at Sunset Beach and the house that his ex-wife still lived in at Garden Grove. The idea was that I could get to both places easily in my car.

Time escaped me and I was more exhausted from the journey than I previously anticipated. It didn't feel right to put myself in front of strangers in that condition, so I decided to drop my bags, grab a drink, drive slowly through the neighbourhood, park up for a while, - and see what, if anything, was going on.

The Sumners' house was located just off the beach on a row of houses, some semi-detached - and some detached, which ran more or less in a straight line. They were the kind of houses you would draw as a child - a little front garden with a path, two windows at the bottom and two at the top. A velux window seemed to be in the roof at the front, indicating a third floor. There were no garages, but cars seemed to be parked on the right side of the road next to the pavement that lead to the gates. I imagined they had large price tags as I walked around the houses to look at the back. I heard children in what seemed to be quite sizeable gardens, which were screened off by high fences or bushes. Most of them had pools and some of them had balconies on the first and second floors, overlooking the sea.

I wandered back to the main street and sat in my car. Far enough away not to seem too obvious but close enough to see. A slim woman of medium height left the house soon after a man arrived. I assumed the man was Richard and the woman, his new wife. She returned about an hour later, looking a little ruffled. Shortly after that the blinds went down in the bottom right room - an office maybe? At around seven, the curtains were drawn in the two top rooms. I decided to drive by the mother's house before returning to my hotel.

I'd managed to get hold of a court report that stated the girl, Chloe, lived here. I was waiting on an old friend to email over some of her medical records from when she was a patient at Great Ormand Street in London. It took a while to organise, because I had to apply for permission to access the records. Bureaucracy gone mad.

The girl's mother, Kate, separated from Richard some five years previously. There were records of her having problems with alcohol and drink driving. In the end, the courts recommended that the girl live with her father and his new wife. Kate had supervised visits twice a week, but I could see that for some time now she only turned up once a fortnight or so.

Kate lived in Garden Grove, which was still in Orange County, but about a twenty-minute drive from Sunset Beach. It was close to Anaheim, which was well known because it homed Disneyland Resort. According to my information, Kate had worked in the offices there for the last twenty years. I imagined they took Chloe as a young girl. I wondered, if she was Grace, why no one had spotted her and reported her as that missing girl from the UK?

Her house seemed modest compared to the Sumner's. It was slightly out of town and looked more like a bungalow than a large family home. There seemed to be a large garden out back with some orange trees, but you couldn't access it. The main part of town was a block or so away - a strip of restaurants and bars, a library, and a children's play area. I wondered how Kate was now, if she was still working, if she was happy? There wasn't a car in the drive, but that didn't mean a lot since Kate's driving licence had been revoked.

Night was drawing in, so I decided to head back to my hotel. I called my mam briefly and then Alice. I switched on my laptop and saw that the medical notes had been sent over. Not before time, I thought to myself, as I clicked open the attachments. Chloe had been admitted for a heart transplant. The operation went well. She was well on the road to recovery when she contracted an infection. The doctors had tried, but the pressure was too much stress for her new heart. She passed away one night in the children's ward with her mother at her side. Kate collected her tiny body five days later. The next day, she booked two seats on a plane back to California. No booking for a coffin. No mention of a body being onboard the aircraft.

I shuddered with excitement as I read the report, hoping that Kate hadn't booked the extra seat simply because she couldn't bear to fly back alone. Why had no one else noticed this? Passport control was a lot less strict back then, but still surely - passports ceased to exist once a person had moved on? A British Passport, yes, I thought to myself, American Passport control wouldn't have a record of any death if they weren't informed by the parents. You wouldn't do that would you, if you were trying to take a different child out of the country, trying to pass her off as someone else.

Chloe Sumner wasn't who everyone thought she was, and that would change everything, even if she wasn't Grace. The real Chloe Sumner had been gone for ten years. The real Chloe Sumner was only a little older than Grace but no doubt, she had been small for her age because of her chronic illness.

This was it - the moment we had all been waiting for. The moment that held so much expectation. I knew I wouldn't sleep much that night, knew I wouldn't rest until I finally had an answer.

We had come so far. This had to be it. It was time for the truth to be revealed. It was time for Grace to come home.

Chapter Twenty Four

Jen, 2006

Ric came out of the office looking like someone else, looking like he had aged ten years in the space of a couple of hours. I'd put the girls to bed. I called Kate. I admit that it wasn't my finest hour, but what else could I have done? We needed answers. I told Kate that we needed to talk, face to face, woman to woman. She didn't seem to object. 6am, I told her at the cafe on the beachfront. Ric and I used to run there in the days before the girls so I knew it opened early. I didn't tell her that though, obviously. I couldn't say anything that might rattle her.

Ric and I talked late into the night about our options, about what we would do, what we could do. The lawyer would be coming at 8am. The girls wouldn't be going to school. I'd call in sick to work. Family emergency. That is what you would call this, isn't it? Maybe even family *in* emergency?

I drifted in and out of sleep in the early hours, as restless as I would expect given the circumstances. I told Ric that I was going for a run and I would be back in an hour. He nodded. I pulled on some shorts and a t-shirt, threw on my old running sneakers that had long since retired. He didn't say anything, didn't seem suspicious.

The morning was fresh and warm. The sun was rising nicely over the water. There weren't that many people about, but that wasn't unusual. It didn't take me long to get there. I ordered two lattes and a large glass of water. I wasn't really sure I could stomach the coffee at all with the rate it was throwing summersaults. The run probably didn't help.

She arrived ten minutes late. Typical really. Nothing was ever a rush for her. She always turned up to contacts late - that was, if she turned up at all. Sometimes I wondered what Chloe really thought about her. She had become indifferent to her mother over the last year. On the days when Kate would be visiting Chloe, we didn't turn up at the contact centre until they had called to say Kate had arrived. I wasn't going to make the poor girl trawl over there and wait for her mother who probably wouldn't show up. They told Kate she could take her out for a day in the holidays if she was supervised. Kate seemed uninterested, unwilling to be watched by someone else.

"This is cosy," Kate said as she took a seat. She didn't look flustered or agitated as she put two sugars in her coffee. I often wondered how she had stayed slim all these years. She certainly didn't work out.

"I picked up a book yesterday - in Wal-mart," I began. She watched me, poised, waiting. "There was a picture of Chloe on the front. Well, a picture of a girl who looks a damn sight like Chloe. But the book was about another little girl. Grace. She went missing ten years ago..."

I let my voice trail off, watched her as her eyes widened. Wondering if she would tell me anything.

"You know, Kate," I continued. "I realise we didn't have the best starts. I took your husband away from you, but we all know that he had long since left you, mentally. You don't like me and that's fair enough, you have every right to your feelings. But I have always loved Chloe. Always treated her no differently than Emily. I've tried to be a good Step-mom. I've tried to make time for her and me to have our own relationship. Not one that will hinder what she has with you, because you are her Mom, and I understand that. She needs someone to look out for her, to care about what she is doing, to know her capabilities, and to understand when something is wrong. This isn't about us now; it's about Chloe, about what is best for her, and how the hell we are going to get out of this mess. I need your help here. Please. I need to know the truth so that we can try to hold onto whatever chance there is of her staying here - with us, with her family."

Kate watched me. She took a deep breath and paused for a long moment. She eyed me with suspicion, probably wondering if I really was someone she could trust.

"I knew that this book would be the end of all this. I'm surprised, really, that I've managed to keep her this long. Ten years. I've been watching the UK news on TV. Her real Mom sure isn't a quitter, isn't willing to let her go. I did what I did in a moment of madness. I've thought about sending her back, handing her over. But how could I? The longer I kept her, the easier the lies became, the more I couldn't give her back. You're a mother now. I'm sure you understand what I'm trying to say. I'll tell you what happened to her, because you deserve the truth. Chloe deserves the truth. But once that's done, I want you to let me go. I've long since gone from this earth, and I have no plans to go through a lengthy trial and prison. I'll never see her again. All the distancing, I did it for her, not for me. Its better that she doesn't have such a good relationship with a woman who brought her up on lies. If you agree, then I'll walk away from here and... I'll do things my own way. You won't be implicated. You might even get to keep her. I don't know...."

I thought for a moment and nodded. "You have my word." I owed her that at least, didn't I? Mother to mother? Woman to woman? Kate took a long sip of her coffee. Then she began to talk.

Chapter Twenty Five

Richard, 2006

Emily woke first at just after seven. She'd always been an early riser, like her mother. It didn't matter what time she went to bed at night, she would be up at the crack of dawn. Emily came and sat at the breakfast bar, poured some Cheerio's into a bowl and wrinkled her nose when I gave her some fresh juice, which she tolerated for us, but didn't really like. An ongoing battle between us wanting what's best and Emily wanting anything but. I told her we were having a stay at home day today and her eyes widened in surprise.

"Are we taking a trip?" she asked with excitement.

"No, honey. Mom might take you out later, but we have to talk to a special lady about some grown-up things this morning. We can't take you to school because Mommy and Daddy need to talk to the lady, and by the time she's gone it's not going to be worth it for you girls to go into to school."

I poured myself a coffee and tried to act normally when I heard Chloe moving around upstairs. Shortly after, she came down in her pyjamas, sleepy and ruffled, sat next to Emily, and grabbed a breakfast bowl.

"We are staying home today," Emily told her. She looked at me for back up while she grabbed the raisin bran.

"Jen and I have someone coming over this morning to talk to us and we don't have time to pool you to school. We thought you could do some work in your room this morning and then we might all go out somewhere this afternoon - the mall, maybe?"

I knew the mall was a good enough lure for her not to ask any questions. Chloe nodded. She didn't seem worried or unsettled by the revelation, but then why should she be? Why did she have any reason not to trust her father? The girls chatted idly about some TV show that was on this morning while I busied myself, trying to tidy up from last night's dinner. The weather was warming up and it was going to be a beautiful day.

Jen arrived back and jumped in the shower. The girls settled themselves at the table in the garden. I imagined they would do a bit of schoolwork before hitting the pool. Chloe was a good swimmer. She was on the swim team at school and was keen on doing extra practice in our rather small pool. She trained after school for an hour most days. Her coach was tough, but Chloe seemed to enjoy the challenge. They were hoping to make the regional finals next semester and the kids had to be at their peak.

I tidied around the kitchen table. We could talk with the doors closed, but be out of the way a little, enough to keep an eye on the girls. Jen felt nervous about the pool, because Emily wasn't as strong a swimmer as her sister.

I felt relieved that my lawyer was coming over so early. She had been good to me during the divorce. I'd wanted to be fair, to let Kate keep the house. I'd wanted as much access as I could have with Chloe, wanted things sorted properly. She managed to make an agreement that suited us both. She stopped things from dragging out, from any bitterness that might have occurred.

Jen busied herself with sorting out some paperwork that our lawyer might want to see – passports, birth certificates, medical records, and copies of the last few years of school results for Chloe. She was a bright, popular girl and was second in her class. Math was her low point, but I took time to help her with it and she had improved a lot over the last year.

At around quarter to eight, the doorbell rang. I walked through and opened the door, expecting my lawyer to be standing there, but instead was greeted by a small, medium build-built man who I'd never seen before.

"Edward Harper," the man introduced himself, holding out his hand. I took it, shaking it cautiously. He showed me a badge that proved he was a private investigator of some kind. I tried to remain calm, to seem unaffected by this man.

"I'm investigating the whereabouts of a missing girl from the United Kingdom – Grace Robinson." He produced the picture that had been sprawled across the front of the book, which remained locked securely in my safe. "May I come in?" he asked.

I stood aside and gestured for him to step into my office. What else could I do? His arrival took me completely by surprise. I could hardly stand there talking about the missing girl on my doorstep, could I? Knowing that in all likelihood the girl was in fact playing quite happily in the back garden, unbeknown to all this drama? That the missing girl was actually *my* daughter.

The man, Edward, launched into a speech about his involvement with the case. He seemed excited, energised. I wondered how his search had led him here when he launched into an explanation of tracking down all children who left the UK by plane or boat in the month after this little girl had gone missing. Kate clearly hadn't been as careful as she had thought. Edward asked to see documents, proving that Chloe belonged here, that Chloe was in fact my daughter. I showed him a copy of her birth certificate that I kept in the top drawer of my desk. I barely listened to his voice as he began speaking about what would happen next. He wanted to see Chloe *'to be sure'* he said. I told him that now wasn't a good time, that Chloe had gone in early to school for swim practice. I was surprised how easily the lie fell off my tongue, how easy it was to lie to protect those I loved the most.

"My wife and I are actually expecting someone shortly," I began telling him as the doorbell rang again, as if on cue. I heard Jen answer it, taking our lawyer into the back room far enough away from my office so that Edward couldn't hear what was going on. "Could you call back this afternoon maybe? Later, when Chloe is back from school? I'm sure that this is all some misunderstanding and it's probably inconvenient for you to wait around all day. But I'd rather not have to pull her out of her training..."

I gave him a card with my number on it and told him that apart from picking up Chloe, we would be here all day. He frowned, but seemed satisfied enough with my answer and thanked me for my time before I showed him to the door. I wondered how much fuel I had just added to the fire. I had no doubt this man would be back later. It was time to get some proper advice. Did this man have any legal power? Could he simply just ask to see Chloe? If I became non-compliant would that implicate me further?

Suddenly, I had a bad feeling in the pit of my stomach that all of this was only the beginning. That before long, we were going to be in this and in it deep. I walked into the kitchen to join Jen and our lawyer. I needed to know how bad this could get.

Chapter Twenty Six

Kate, 2006

There is always something in your life that you want to keep hidden from others. For most people, it's usually something silly, something you did when you were a child or a teenager. Smoking behind the bike sheds, or staying somewhere else when you said you were with a friend. Something that isn't important in the grand scheme of life.

But there are another group of people with real problems to hide – criminals or crime victims, usually. Maybe their father was a murderer or a rapist? Maybe a situation went too far and a crime was committed? Maybe they just overlooked something - didn't put the stair gate up in time, didn't watch the toddler as she grabbed the hot kettle?

I came to the USA to escape from something I wanted to keep hidden. My father was a man with power, a man who let his mind rule his body. He was, I know now, an abuser. I was the abused.

My mother was weak and unable to calm him, unable to stop him from doing *bad things*. I know that he went after other young girls, other children. He picked them up in play areas, outside of secondary schools. Eventually, he was caught in a bad situation and he was imprisoned. The real truths of all his crimes were laid bare for all to see. Other victims came forward with their stories. No less than eight girls in total. They wanted justice to be sought and I know they deserved that, at least, after what he had done to them. A fellow prisoner of my father's managed to finish him off within the same year he was sent down. No one likes someone who messes with children. Not even murderers.

After he was gone, we were given new identities, new names. We moved to a different part of the country, a part where no one knew who we were and what we were hiding. I was the quiet girl at school. I liked to blend in. My mother got a little job in a supermarket. She never met anyone else. I thought that she couldn't bear it. The thought of another man turning out like my father.

I worked hard at school and I left the UK soon afterwards and found a good life in America. I got married. But the children never came. Time and time again they became 'lost'. *"I'm sorry, Mrs. Sumner,"* they said, *"but you have lost your baby."* I never liked it - that word, *lost*. Lost implies carelessness, thoughtlessness. Children are precious. If I were blessed with one, I would never do such a thing. I would never leave it alone for more than a moment. I would always make sure it was safe and loved. I would never *lose* a baby. Not like that, not the way the word implies. The 'losing' was beyond my control. I couldn't do anything about it.

It began to consume me, this need to have children. So many lost babies. Richard was ready to give up when I fell pregnant with Chloe. We didn't dare speak about it. Didn't dare get excited. We'd done that too many times before. The first time, we decorated the nursery, put up the cot. We called everyone we knew and told them the good news. For many years now, the door to the nursery remained firmly shut. We became wiser to it, the hope. We tried not to have expectations.

Then, in a flurry of excitement, she arrived. So beautiful and precious. Yet, so vulnerable, so ill and sickly. Ric found it hard to bond with her. I wondered if we should get too attached to her - a child that could easily end up on the *lost* pile. Yet, of course, you do - her smile, her laughter. We did everything we could for her tiny, failing heart. I knew that taking her to London could ruin many things – our marriage being the main one. But I couldn't lose her. Couldn't live the rest of my life knowing I had put my marriage and myself before my daughter. That isn't what a good parent would do, is it? That isn't the right thing to do for your child.

I took her to London on my own. I walked her to the operating room. I held her hand as she woke up, held her little helpless body through all the wires. I told her everything would be okay and I almost believed it would be, until the night when all the buzzers went off when everyone else was sleeping. The night that they tried and failed to bring her back. The night that a large piece of myself died with her. The night that left me broken.

I couldn't call Ric. Truth be told, I couldn't speak to anyone. I took my hire car and drove out of the city. I drove towards the sea – Brighton, Portsmouth, Weymouth. I checked into small bed and breakfasts for one night only. The owners asked about the baby seat in the rear of the car. *'She's in the hospital, recovering,'* I would tell them, and *'I need a night of unbroken sleep, because of all those buzzers.'* They didn't question me too much. People don't like to hear that tiny children are sick and dying. It makes them question the world too much, makes them wonder: why them? Why are little innocent children allowed to be so gravely ill when murderers are still alive? I didn't expand on my story; I didn't need to. I wandered aimlessly throughout the different towns, anonymous, trying to get a handle on my grief before I made that call to my husband. The call that would destroy him, destroy us.

I was going to stop in Plymouth one day, but couldn't bring myself to do it, so I kept on driving to Cornwall. I believed I was being punished for my father's mistakes. That karma came to those who least expected it. In Cornwall, I checked into another little bed and breakfast. I went through the same questions, the same answers. I was barely aware of what the place was called, in my haze. Perranporth, I know now. That quaint, little seaside village. So beautifully natural, with that long, sandy beach. The little shops in a row on the main street, and the little boating lake. It wasn't hard to see why this was a popular holiday destination. Chloe would have loved it.

Arriving in Perranporth was an act that was so innocent, unintentional. I didn't plan to take someone else's baby. I didn't think that, because my baby was gone, I was entitled to a replacement. I must tell you that I never meant to take the baby. She was just there as I was driving by, on my way out of the village the next morning. Alone, in her pushchair, and fast asleep. I believed it was fate. When I unbuckled her, she didn't even stir or whimper. She didn't struggle. She was quiet and peaceful.

I slipped her into the car seat, strapped her in, and drove off.

Chapter Twenty Seven

Jen, 2006

Sat in my own kitchen, I've never felt so nervous. Ric looks as bad as I feel. He is twitching his hands, and fiddling with a piece of paper and a pencil. I can see the girls laughing and playing in the pool. Emily squirting Chloe with a water gun; Chloe giving her a brief moment of victory.

We outlined what we know to Ric's solicitor – Armstrong is her surname. Ric and I joked about her in the past. *'She sure takes one giant leap for mankind,'* he said. Louise is her first name. She seems relatively un-phased, unworried. I imagined she would feel a lot more worried, though, if this happened to her family, if she discovered that her child really belonged to someone else.

Louise tells us we are innocent bystanders to this whole charade. Our defence is: we never knew the truth. Cooperation with the authorities would be better for us, she says. Let them take DNA from Chloe to ascertain who she belongs to. Call this woman in England, her possible birth mother. Talk to her; let her know that she is safe and loved. Play nice; let her come and see for herself. Don't let them come marching in with an order for arrest and a warrant to remove her and send her on the first plane back to England. Do not talk to anyone about anything. Do not let the private investigator - that Ric had answered the door to - back in. We'll deal with the authorities and the mother only on our terms.

Most importantly, she stressed - as she was leaving, promising to come back later on - we need to sit Chloe down and tell her the truth. The solicitor made all of this seem so simple, as if telling your daughter that she was once kidnapped, and actually belongs to someone else, were an everyday occurrence. I was worried about what it would do to her, what it would do to our family. Worried about how a child would cope with being told that everything she believed was actually a lie. That she had this whole other life, before. That she had a birth mother out there who wanted her back.

I watched Ric as he sat her down in the living room. He showed her the copy of the book I had picked up in Wal-mart. He explained, cautiously, that it might be possible that she is the girl who was taken, all those years ago. He told her that some people would be coming over to take some of her DNA to make sure, to see if she really was this missing girl, Grace Robinson. He told her it didn't matter what the test said; that she was our daughter and we would do everything we could to keep her here with us.

"This woman... - is she nice?" she asked, curious, I suppose, of the new stranger who suddenly could be her mother.

"We haven't spoken to her – yet," Ric told her. "Her name is Alice. The solicitor is sorting out the DNA test, which they will fast track, and they will see if it is a match to her other daughter, Hope. The girl that went missing was an identical twin. Maybe Alice will come over here - to visit. It depends on how the British authorities want to go about it. If they want to get tough, it could get difficult..." he trailed off.

Chloe nodded. She seemed confused, but not too distraught. I wondered what I expected her to do – break down, and throw plates at the wall? It would have been so unlike her. She was usually very composed. I wondered how much the truth really hurt her, how she managed to stay so calm. Later, I would be glad that Ric talked to her then, that we were given an opportunity to make her less afraid of what would follow. Unbeknown to us, it was already out of our hands. We were little fish in a big pond. Try as we might, we couldn't keep our family safe.

Chapter Twenty Eight

Edd, 2006

I'd managed to create a bit of a fluster with my unannounced visit. Richard Sumner was surprised and taken aback by my presence. He didn't seem particularly overwhelmed by anything I told him, which meant one of two things: 1) He knew that Chloe wasn't Chloe, and knew exactly who she was and where she came from; or 2) He knew Chloe wasn't Chloe, but the news of this was somewhat of a revelation to him.

I wasn't sure which category he fell into, but his prompt production of her birth certificate (the one that I knew meant nothing) led me to believe he knew something and he was keen for that something to be hidden, for it to only be disclosed on his own terms. The trouble in my mind was that it wasn't his place to be dictating anything or calling any shots.

I called Chloe's school to see what time her swim practice finished, only to be told there was no swim practice this morning and I must have been misinformed. I had a very bad feeling that this wouldn't be simple. I wondered for a moment what to do next. I didn't think I could wait until I knocked on the door again later in the day. I had a very strong suspicion that my next visit wouldn't be so welcome, that I would be lucky if anyone even answered the door, let alone let me inside.

If I could just get a glimpse of Chloe. I'd spent a lot of time with Hope over the years. I always carried the most recent picture of her in my wallet, just in case. If I could just see her for a passing moment, I was sure I would know the truth.

I drove back to Chloe's mother's house in Garden Grove - Kate Sumner's. Again, she wasn't in, and there were no signs of activity as I peered into a couple of windows. The house must have been lived in, as there was lived-in clutter around the place. It wasn't untidy yet it wasn't immaculate either. There was unopened mail on the hall table. Something told me she had just up and left at some point, probably fairly recently. Maybe she saw a copy of the book somewhere? Maybe she knew her time was up, that she was close to being caught after all these years? Maybe she jumped ship before she was pushed?

I decided to take a chance by knocking on the door of the house next door. A young-ish woman opened it, holding a toddler. I explained my reason for being in the area. I asked her if she had any recent pictures of Kate's daughter, Chloe.

"We had a BBQ a couple of months back and Chloe came with Ric and Emily," she began. "She used to play with my girls, you know, when she lived here permanently. She was a nice girl... Kate tends to keep to herself these days. I know she doesn't get to see her much anymore, with one thing and another... Anyway, I'm sure there will be a picture somewhere on the computer..."

She directed me to a desk with a PC on it, and turned it on. As she clicked through the photographs, my heart began to race. It only took her a few moments to find it, the picture of Chloe. I stared at the girl. Her skin was darker than Hope's, but her eyes were the same shade of blue. Her hair was cut shorter. There was absolutely no doubt in my mind - that we had just found Grace.

Chapter Twenty Nine

Kate, 2006

I decided long ago that when this moment came, I would simply disappear. It doesn't really seem fair though, I know. I committed a crime and I should be accountable for it. The trouble is, I couldn't face prison. I'd wither and die in there. I'd be like my father. Perhaps, I wouldn't be killed, but people would think badly of me. I am not a criminal as such, although I do know that's what people are going to think of me.

Sometimes, I like to think of myself as a misguided soul. I meant to give her back over the years, back to her real family. Leave her somewhere with a note or something. That happens, doesn't it? I didn't mean to keep her. But as time went on, I couldn't do it - she became *my* daughter so easily. Ric didn't suspect a thing. People called her our little miracle: *'so healthy now,'* they would say, and *'you'd never know that she'd been such a sick little girl.'* Of course they thought that, and of course they never knew that Chloe didn't look sick anymore because she never had been. Our new daughter was blessed with her own tiny, perfect heart.

Alice Winters is a mother to be reckoned with. I thought she would have given up looking for Grace years ago. I kept my eye on her, looked at copies of British Newspapers in the public library, and searched the internet for new information. She remarried and has a son now too. Two children, I thought to myself when I found out. Another child would give her three, and leave me with nothing. Selfish, I know. The trouble was, that although I knew Chloe wasn't mine, biologically, she became mine. The trouble was, it felt right; I felt I deserved her and that she deserved a good life with us. We would never be so careless to leave her alone like her father had done. We would be the best parents for her.

But as time went on, bad thoughts began to creep in. Drinking took the edge off them, made me think that keeping her was all right, when I was having a moment of guilt. The older she became, the more guilt I felt, and the more I drank.

Eventually, Richard left me for someone else, and I couldn't blame him. He never hid the fact that he wanted Chloe with them, and we went to court for custody. I won, but it was only a matter of time before things got out of hand, out of my control. I was picked up by the police when I was in the wagon one morning, and I knew that was it. I told myself that she would be better off with them, with Richard, his new wife, and their baby. I told myself that when the truth came out, the authorities might be more lenient with Richard and Jen - a happy, secure, little family who hadn't really done anything wrong. Whereas, I didn't have a chance in hell.

The police had taken my licence off me for the drinking incident, but I was allowed it back after some time of 'good behaviour'. I needed a car for work, I pleaded. I needed a car to get to the contact centre without having to catch three separate busses. The courts relented and let me have it back. Any sign of bad behaviour, I was warned that it would be revoked again, faster than the speed of light.

I bought a camper van with cash, in my new name, in a different city. I bought a little car that I left in the driveway. I stored the van somewhere safe, and bought the things I needed to hit the road and cross state. I let myself go a bit and I had become quite fat. I let people take pictures of my fatter self when I went to dinner parties and functions.

Then I went on a rapid diet three months before Alice's book was due to be released. I became a social recluse - had the shopping delivered to the house. I wore baggy jumpers for work, saved up all of my holidays and took the last month off work completely. I was so sure the book would mark the end for us. So sure, in fact, that I was ready to go as soon as the publication over here became a reality.

Long, long ago, I decided the disappearing part would be easy. I saved up cash. I moved some money into a different account, an account in my maiden name. I planned to take the van for a few weeks until things died down with the press. Then I'd go back to the United Kingdom. I'd make sure that Chloe was okay, from a distance. I'd get a job with my new identity.

People do it more than you think, you know - go on the run. You just need to know how to find the people who can provide you with all the paperwork – a new social security number, birth certificate, and passport. You need to have enough money, cash preferably. These people don't ask questions, don't seem to care what you're doing, so long as you pay up. A couple of weeks later and you can become a completely new person. Just like that. So simple.

I wanted people to believe that I was gone for good, and that was the trickiest part of my movements to coordinate. There was a bad bit of coast road on the edge of a high hill, the scenic route back from where an old friend lived. I planned to go late at night and drive my car off – jumping out at the last moment. I planned to fill my car with shopping and gas, because who would spend over a hundred dollars on groceries before killing themselves? It wasn't logical.

I would call my old friend and tell her I would pop over for a coffee after I had been shopping. I was sure she would alert the police when I hadn't shown up for a few hours. The car would be a wreck, but it would look like an accident – as if I went a little too fast, too close to the edge and tumbled down the embanking. However, I'd be long gone before they realised who I really was and what I'd done. That was the plan.

I met with Jen this morning. She is a woman I grew to like, though I never really had the chance to know her properly. It's not what you do, is it, with your ex-husband's new wife? There's supposed to be animosity. I knew she thought I was a bad mother, and I suppose that she was right, with the distancing I tried to do with Chloe. I wanted my disappearance to be easier for Chloe to deal with, and me turning up to all those supervised contacts would make it far worse for her in the long-term.

I told Jen as much of the truth as I dared I could tell her without her implicating herself or Ric. I told her she was a good mother and to take care of her, to keep her safe. She pleaded with me to stay, to work things out. I told her no, it has to be like this; it is the only way. I let her believe that I wanted to die. I told her what I did with the real Chloe, for Ric more than anything. He's the kind of man who needs closure on things. Not knowing would have been unnecessary torment for him – unneeded and unfounded. I told Jen it was time for me to go. I told her to tell Chloe that I was sorry and that loved her.

I'm sitting in the car now. I've done the shopping and it's loaded into the trunk of the car. I wore a wig for the cameras in the supermarket, but I took it off once I reached the car. I also changed my clothes. I threw everything I wore in a dumpster. In many ways, it reminded me of what I did with Grace all those years ago: stopping in the lay-by and cutting her hair, stopping at the supermarket and buying the things I would need to take care of her - properly. But now, my new life will begin the moment I drive away from this car park. I am as ready as I ever will be. I started the engine and left.

Chapter Thirty

Alice, 2006

I received the call. Years and years I waited for this moment. Years and years of wonder, years of trying. I place the phone down and breathe. I counted to five. I smiled. We did it, I thought to myself. All that work, all the campaigning, and writing of the book. We did what was needed to bring her home.

It was worth every second to hear the voice of a US police officer. *'We have strong evidence to suggest that we have located your missing daughter, Grace.'* Those were his exact words. I didn't correct him; I didn't tell him it was actually Edd who put all the pieces together. That it was Edd who was the only one looking with grit and determination for all these years. It was Edd who had called the United States Police and Interpol. Edd who made all the links, off his own back. *'We are waiting for a positive DNA before we take any action,'* he explained to me a few hours ago.

They arrested the 'father'. They issued the step-mother with a court order not to remove Grace from the state of California for the few hours before the arrest took place. The British consulate would see Grace returned to me with *'immediate effect.'* Edd would be with her during the flight. In less than forty-eight hours, Grace would be home.

I called Tom at work and he cancelled his appointments for the afternoon and came home, collecting Ethan and Hope on the way. We sat them down in the living room and told them that Grace had been found, she was well, and she was coming home. Ethan was slightly confused about the whole matter, but then, he was only six years old. It's a hard concept to grasp. Hope took it in her stride, asking more appropriate questions like: *'Will she remember us?'* I told her probably not, and it's better not to expect too much from her to begin with. Although she belongs to us, this will be a big shock and a big change for her to adapt to. We will have to try to do everything we can to make her feel at home with us. To make her understand that we are her family and we love her.

The story will run front page of the national newspapers in the morning. I wished that they would wait until she is settled, but I could hardly dictate to them. They were so helpful in those early days - with getting her picture out there. They were helpful too, in the run up to my book, giving exclusive interviews and running the most recent picture of Hope. Tom pulled all the phones out. We asked the press for privacy, for Grace to settle back into a normal life with us, before we have the interviews they are so desperate for – that after everything that had happened, she was still just a child.

Tom and I discussed the practicalities of having Grace back with us – taking time off work being the main thing. I wanted to fly out to California to collect her myself, but it would just delay her arrival to us. We would collect her from the airport where she was being chaperoned by a woman from American Social Services and Edd, who I spoke to on the phone. Edd told me that Chloe, as she was now known, had been quiet but compliant. She'd packed some things from the house into a suitcase and showed no resistance. She became upset saying goodbye to her sister and step-mother, who she lived with in a nice area of town near the beach. It was understandable, I suppose. But I found that quite difficult to deal with. Difficult to understand.

The exact details of the kidnapping wouldn't be clear until they questioned the parents and the investigation was well underway, but Grace had been well cared for and loved in her time without us. She was bright and athletic. There were no signs of neglect, ill treatment or anything sinister. Silent tears ran down my face as the officer relayed this information to me. It's what I had wanted and wished for all of these years. That she was happy and loved.

I called everyone we knew to tell them the good news – my father, my brothers, Jack's parents. I told them that we would allow Chloe time to settle in before bombarding her with the rest of the family, and they happily agreed. Nothing mattered now that we knew she was safe. Nothing mattered now that we were getting her back, because we had all the time in the world to make up for the time we had already lost.

Hope and I tidied up her room together. Tom was out buying her a laptop so she could keep in touch with her friends from school. It was a small thing that I overlooked, but it would become invaluable to Grace. She needed to embrace her new life with us, but we couldn't let all of her ties with her old one to be cut – it would be cruel and unnecessary. We talked about how much they would be the same – Hope and Grace. I explained to Hope that although they were the same genetically, Grace lived for many years with different people in a different country. She would probably be quite different personality wise; probably like different things and dress differently. I didn't want Hope to have the wrong ideas, to think they would be identical in every sense. They couldn't be, after all those years apart.

Ethan made a banner saying 'Welcome home,' and we stretched it over the front door of the house. It seemed the right thing to do. We would have a little party in the house, our little family of five. A special dinner, something that we didn't usually have. I was as happy and nervous as I could be, at the same time. It was all falling into place for us. From here on in, it would all be easy, wouldn't it?

Chapter Thirty One

Richard, 2006

We barely had time to breathe after my solicitor left before the door went again. Jen took some snacks to the girls outside, so I wandered through to the hallway to answer it. I found two police officers standing there. Who had sent them? I wondered, as I let them into my office. I told them I wanted my wife to be present at this *'informal discussion,'* which is what they called it. As calmly as I could, I left them to find Jen and warn her what was happening. Her eyes widened when I told her they were sitting in my office, and we walked back there together, silently.

Jen knew one of the officers from the area. He had a diabetic cat that was in her clinic on a fairly regular basis. They apologised for having to come. *'Didn't seem right'* one of them said before the other launched into an explanation. I supposed it didn't seem right that something like this could happen in our otherwise quiet neighbourhood.

"Richard Sumner, we have received a notice from the British Police that you are harbouring a child taken from a village in Cornwall in 1996." The officer Jen knew rolled his eyes. The other officer continued, "In order to verify this information we need to take a sample of DNA from Chloe Sumner right this moment. We have a warrant..." he pushed the piece of paper forwards for Jen to examine. She nodded her approval that the paperwork was correct.

"The chief investigating officer doesn't want anything going further until the results of the DNA test is back from the lab. However, we also have a court order here that stops you from taking your children out of California in the meantime. You should also be aware that we have an unmarked vehicle watching your house, so please don't think of making any rash decisions. We hope this is all a misunderstanding and we can go back to our daily lives and jobs. You are well-regarded in the community; your children are well-known to be loved and well cared for. You may or may not wish to talk to Chloe about this; we will leave that to your own discretion...."

His voice trailed off. I gave Jen a quick look. They must have had a tip off? They must believe they are correct in their assumptions, otherwise, why send officers over here? Why have an unmarked car in our street?

We took the officers out the back. Jen explained to Chloe what they were doing and she nodded. They took a sample of her hair and it was relatively simple and pain free, for Chloe at least. I realised there would be no terms to dictate anymore with the authorities involved and it worried me. Social Services had a bad track record for the last few years, and as such, they liked to jump in when it wasn't always needed. It happened to a boy I had in my math class – they put him in foster care quicker than you can order McDonald's at the drive thru.

The officers seemed to leave satisfied. They would be back later, because they would be fast-tracking the DNA results, they said, as they were departing. Jen told them we would be in all afternoon. Really, though, what choice did we have? We could hardly do anything when we were being watched, and being followed.

I called Louise Armstrong, my solicitor, and she agreed to come back over earlier than we had planned. *'Try not to worry'* she said.

Less than two hours later, though, the police officers were back as promised. This time with a warrant for arrest.

Chapter Thirty Two

Edd, 2006

The American Police turned out to be most helpful. I briefed another officer the outline of the story surrounding Grace. The British Authorities were keen to get Chloe's DNA and have her brought back to England at the earliest available opportunity. The US allowed an immediate warrant and for the test to be fast-tracked. They agreed that with backup and a positive DNA result, I would be allowed to go in and take Chloe to police custody until a flight could be scheduled.

The next couple of hours seemed to drag, as I retold as much information I thought was necessary to the case. When the DNA came back positive, the first thing I did was call Alice. *'We are going in to remove her; an officer will call you with more information as soon as it is available. I'll take good care of her, Alice. I promise.'*

We sped through the neighbourhood in three cars back to the Sumner's. Richard looked distraught as they cuffed him and put him in the back of a police van. I wondered how thoroughly they would interview him, how long it would take him to be able to get his own legal advice. I felt a twinge of sympathy for him, though I knew that I shouldn't. He loved Chloe, I was certain of it. Wrong as his actions may have been, she hadn't come to any harm as such, hadn't lived a bad life. I could only hope for the same for my own brother, Alan, though I knew that really it was a lot more unrealistic.

I followed as the police walked into the garden. Richards's wife was comforting the younger girl who was sobbing for her father. Chloe sat next to her, wide-eyed and afraid.

"We have come here today, Chloe, because the test we took earlier tells us that you really do belong to someone else. The police in the United Kingdom want you to be taken back to them while all of this...other stuff... - is sorted out..." an officer explained.

"When can I see my dad?" she asked.

"You'll probably be able to talk to Richard as soon as he is released from police custody, depending on what he tells the police. You'll be going back to England, so I don't know when you'll see him next...."

She nodded and turned to Jen and Emily, burying her face in Jen's t-shirt. I didn't think she was crying, she just needed a moment to comfort herself, to work through her thoughts.

"We need you to go and pack anything you think you might need, Chloe. It's a long flight. Would you like Jen to help you?"

Chloe nodded, apprehensively.

Jen straightened herself and took both girls by the hand, leading them back inside. She struck me as a woman who wouldn't fall apart in front of her children. As a woman who did a job that had to be done, however unpleasant it may seem to her or how wrong she thought it might be. I had no doubt the Sumner's would fight for Chloe. They would give everything they had, emotionally and financially, for her to return to them. I wondered fleetingly if they would have a strong enough case to have Chloe back here. I worried what that might do to Alice, as we climbed up the stairs. Things never are as simple as they seem.

Chapter Thirty Three

Jen, 2006

It's funny when you can pinpoint a moment that created such devastation. It's funny what your mind lets you remember and what it decides to shut out, for your own sake, so that you can try to carry on with your life in the best way you can.

This is what I remember from this afternoon. The police knocking on the door and entering, in an orderly kind of fashion which seemed strange given the circumstances? There was no shouting, no door being kicked down. Then the officer threw handcuffs on Ric.

"Richard Sumner, we are arresting you for the suspected abduction of Grace Robinson from Cornwall, England in 1996. You do not have to say anything, but it may harm your defence if you do not mention something when questioned that you later rely on in court..."

I remember the look on Ric's face as the other officers were entering our house, looking for Chloe. "Daddy!" I heard Emily cry, and I ran to contain her. A man was telling Chloe what happened and asking her to pack her bag. She was still in her swimsuit. Chloe asked in a pleading voice, when she could see her father. I realised quite quickly that I had to be the strong one here, the one in control. I couldn't show fear or hesitation. I couldn't let Chloe think this was the end of it, that we would just let her go so easily - let her be taken.

We went upstairs to her room to pack some of her things. The investigator was loitering on the landing. Chloe went through her clothes, drawer by drawer, putting in a good mixture of clothes, sleep suits, underwear, a couple of dresses, and some shoes. She threw in the old bear, the bear she had since she was a toddler – who was, in fact, rather un-originally called 'bear.' These days, she tried to pretend that bear didn't matter so much to her, but I noticed she still slipped it into her bag for sleepovers and vacations. I wondered, to myself, if Emily would be the same as she grew up.

"What will happen now?" she asked me in almost a whisper.

"It looks like they are going to send you to the UK..... You'll have to sit tight for a while but we'll work it out. You'll be back here before we know it," I told her.

My answer seemed to satisfy her. I gave her my mobile from my pocket and told her to keep it with her, that we would be able to call her more easily that way. Chloe was thrilled to be given my new all-singing, all-dancing phone. Ric and I had mixed feelings about children having mobiles and he had told Chloe that she wasn't allowed one until she was fifteen, which seemed a bit extreme to me. It seemed irrelevant that it was on a contract. I threw in the charger from our room as an afterthought, and gave her all the cash that was in the nightstand – just over a hundred dollars. I wasn't sure if they would try to block all communication between her and us, but it would be worth the risk if they didn't - and let her keep it. I also didn't want her to have to ask for money from strangers. I told her I was giving her an advance on her allowance, that she might need it.

Emily was still subdued, hanging around me like a limpet, not wanting to be left anywhere that she couldn't see us. I'd have to try to explain all of this to her later on, give her an edited version of what was been happening in our house. With the bags packed, the investigator was keen to get going. I wondered where they were taking her before they managed to book her on a flight. I wondered who would be accompanying her.

We reached the door and Chloe grabbed her coat off the rack and her sneakers off the floor. She made a bit of a drama about putting them on. I didn't have the heart to tell her to hurry. The investigator nodded to me.

"We will take good care of her...." he said, as he opened the door. Chloe was hugging Emily, telling her she would call her, telling her not to worry. She hugged me for a second too long, and I was worried my emotions might get the better of me.

"Be safe.... You can call us anytime, on any day. We will miss you but love you and we *will* see you soon. I promise." Chloe nodded, fighting back the tears now. She was led gently to the door and it was closed behind her.

Just like that, she was gone.

Chapter Thirty Four

Edd, 2006

I wondered what to say to Grace as we drove away from the house in silence. Tears were falling down her cheeks, but she wasn't sobbing, wasn't shouting, or resisting. It seemed to make matters worse. As much as I had wanted this day to come for Alice, I hadn't really spared any consideration for how a child would take this sudden revelation.

We were taking her to a station on the other side of town. The American Authorities wanted to ask her some informal questions about Kate and Richard. The police didn't want to push her - or make her any more uncomfortable than she was already feeling. I suppose they needed to gather any information they could so they could decide how to charge them for her abduction.

After a while, Chloe began tapping on a mobile phone that she'd dug out of her pocket. I'd turned away when I saw Jen give it to her. She needed to have contact with her friends, needed to have contact with people she loved and trusted. Though I realised that Ric and Jen probably had plans to keep in touch with her on it and maybe that shouldn't be allowed, I wondered, what harm would it do? You can't punish a child for an adult's mistakes.

We arrived at the station and were led to an informal interview room. One of the officers got Grace a coke. I was having trouble calling her by her new name. My mind had been calling her Grace for so long that it wasn't happy with changing it to something else.

The police didn't seem to have such problems. To them Grace, or Chloe, was a typical all-American girl. Her old name didn't really suit her. I wondered what the Smith's would call her, if they would change her surname and get all new documentation for her. The passport she held as Chloe Sumners certainly couldn't be legal, though the officials seemed not to be bothered by this technicality.

They asked Grace some questions about her mother and father, about her life as a child – where she had been and what had she done. They asked her if she remembered Hope and her parents. She shook her head. I remembered reading a research article about the age at which most people can recollect real childhood memories. Was it five they had concluded? I couldn't remember. Hope had had her share of problems with dealing with her missing sister, though I did sometimes wonder if she remembered Grace, or remembered the stories Alice had told her.

Grace asked them when she would be coming back to the US, back to her father and step-mother. The officer couldn't quite meet her eye and told her there was *'a lot of legal paperwork to complete first.'* I wondered if it would have been kinder not to give her a real answer. As far as I could see, she wouldn't be returning any time soon.

The British Embassy had booked us both on a plane that flew direct from LAX into Heathrow, London. It was an overnight plane operated by Virgin Atlantic. We would be escorted to the aircraft doors by the police. We had been put in first class seats and I wondered if they had done that to make themselves look better, over-considering our needs. Alice, Tom, Hope, and Ethan would be waiting at the airport to greet us. I hoped there hadn't been too much news leakage and that we wouldn't be bombarded by the press on our arrival.

I'd have to try and talk to Grace on the plane. Alleviate her fears. Make her understand that things will be okay in the end, and that she shouldn't be afraid, shouldn't worry about Richard or what would be happening to him at the station. It was going to be easier said than done.

Chapter Thirty Five

Richard, 2006

I've been sitting in an empty cell for what seems like forever. A parking ticket and speeding fine are the closest I'd come to dealing with the law. I don't think I've ever gone beyond that front desk before.

I'm not perfect. I don't think anyone really is. My parents gave me a very liberal approach to childhood. They told me to *take my own risks* and *follow my dreams*. All good and well, isn't it? But you can't follow your dreams when you have a family to support and bills to pay. We had lived in a rougher area of town so that my dad could earn less money, which allowed him to focus on writing his fantasy novels. Dragons and vampires, that kind of thing. I wanted a better life for myself and for my own family. I worked hard at college. I now have a good job. Eventually, my father's books sold relatively well. They gave up working and took off to see the world. The last time I heard from my mom, they were in Canada, hiking in some national park or other. They had a perfect marriage, but they didn't blame me when mine collapsed.

I know some of the officers who work in the station, through passing. I teach math to some of their children in high school. Some of them know Jen. We would say hello if we passed them on the sidewalk - or on the beach. I am sure they thought I was just an *ordinary* man. I wondered if that's what they thought about other criminals before their crimes became apparent. The people who walk into schools and open fire on kids. The people who get involved in a hit and run accident. Afterwards, they always make the perpetrators look bad – of course Joe Blogs couldn't have committed *that* crime, when he had an ordinary life, an ordinary job, when he volunteered at the homeless shelter. Joe Blogs must have problems, mental health problems. That's what the police like you to believe. How would they categorise me, though? Did they see me as the villain or as the victim?

Eventually, an officer came to my cell and led me to an interview room. The room was bare – a table, a few papers, some video recording equipment. The investigator introduced himself as Banks. He asked me if I wanted a coffee. I asked him if I needed a lawyer.

"We can start now and you can hope that you might get bailed, or we can wait until your solicitor shows up... Louise Armstrong, right? She may take time in rush hour but chances are that she's already on her way over here. I'll have the desk call her and then we can begin without her?" Banks suggested. It didn't seem like I had many options. It didn't seem that leaving here tonight would be a possibility, not at this late stage in the day, no matter how innocent I think I may be.

I told him to go ahead. He began with the normal questions. How had I met Kate? Why did we end up in California? He started asking more uncomfortable questions then: How many babies had we lost? Did we have counselling, IVF? How did we cope when after all those years, we had a baby that was *ill?*

As much as I could, I gave him the truth. I told him that when Chloe arrived, her illness seemed insignificant at first. Trivial almost. I told him that Kate had taken her to the UK for the transplant, and that I had stayed at home. The look in his eyes told me what he was thinking – that I'd let my wife travel halfway across the world with a sick toddler by herself. That I'd let her go through it all alone. I wondered about this myself over the years; wondered if my actions had caused Kate to begin her downward spiral of depression and alcohol misuse. I told him about our separation, that finding out Chloe biologically belonged to another man gave me the courage to leave. That I loved my daughter and that, though the truth was painful, I wouldn't walk out on her, wouldn't leave her without a father.

Banks told me they had done a brief physical examination on Chloe. There was no scar on her chest to indicate any surgery. As I told him that she had been self-conscious of being undressed from a very young age, I realised I was just repeating a lie I had been told. That Kate must have drummed into her repeatedly that you only take off t-shirts and swimsuits when you're on your own. I'd seen her back a couple of times, sure. I wondered if I had seen nothing, no scar, if I'd be in this position today.

I explained to Banks how Chloe had been returned to us – Jen and I. I explained the difficulties we had with Kate over the last couple of years – her disinterest in engaging with her daughter. I told him that less than twenty-four hours ago Jen had picked up the book - and that we had pieced together bits of the truth. That I had tried repeatedly to get hold of Kate with no joy.

Another officer came in and whispered something in Banks' ear. I watched as his eyes widened in surprise.

"What would you say, Richard, if I told you that the only way we can verify anything you have just told me would be to talk to Kate? But unfortunately, Kate's car has just been found at the bottom of a cliff road where it has landed in the ocean. No sign of her body *yet,* but there are divers at the scene. Mightily convenient for you, Richard, wouldn't you say?"

I said nothing.

"We'll take a break. Twenty minutes."

I was taken back to my empty cell.

Chapter Thirty Six

Edd, 2006

Chloe and I boarded our plane with a surprising lack of drama. The only information I had been given by the US police was minimal – that Richard was still being questioned, and the whereabouts of his ex-wife and Chloe's 'mother' were, as yet, unknown.

I let Chloe sit in the window seat. She was curiously interested in looking out of the window at all times, rather than engaging in any discussions with me, or anyone else for that matter. The airhostess brought us the usual kind of aeroplane lunch, and she picked at hers, while I devoured mine. I hadn't eaten in several hours.

"They're showing the new Harry Potter film after lunch," I told her.

For the first time she smiled.

"I've ordered a copy of *Deathly Hallows*.... Maybe I'll have to ask Jen to send it out to me..." Chloe let her voice trail off, as she once again began to think of who she had left behind.

"I know that Hope likes the Harry Potter books too. I'm sure Alice can get another book added to her order. There are a few months left, aren't there? Until it's released?" I asked Chloe, relieved that *finally* I'd broken down the walls of communication.

"Yeah, I guess.... It kind of sucks a bit though. I'm sure that my dad, or Richard, or whatever I'd call him now... - well he didn't do anything *wrong* did he? This all seems a bit *unnecessary*..."

I half-shrugged my shoulders at her.

"The trouble is that you do have a family who have missed you for all these years. You were wrongly taken. I know that this is a bit strange for you.... It'll be hard for you to adjust to a new life. Alice and Tom are good people. I doubt that they're going to stop you having a relationship with your other family."

Chloe nodded, glumly.

"The film is going to start now. Are you watching it or what?" she asked me.

I smiled and put on my headphones. We were five hours away from our destination. Five hours from the Smith's having their precious daughter returned. Five hours from Chloe having to adapt to a completely new country, a completely new life. I wondered, who was going to have the most difficulty adjusting?

Chapter Thirty Seven

Jen, 2006

It's late in the evening and Ric still isn't home. I don't really know why I'm surprised. The police were hardly just going to ask a few questions and set him free. This is going to be a high-profile case. I know that. Our lives are going to become difficult. People are going to whisper as I drop Emily off at kindergarten and talk about us behind our backs. They will think bad things about us - things that we don't deserve.

I've been calling the station every hour. The man on the desk seems to be getting annoyed with my requests for information. Ric's solicitor is with him now. Louise is a headstrong woman, she will do what she can. Will it be enough? I don't know.

On and off, I toy with the idea of going down to the police station. I cook dinner. I put Emily to bed. I call my mom and ask her to come over. She tells me they've found Kate's car; that it's only a matter of time before the body is washed up on the beach - that they had people down there, looking for her.

I decided there and then that it was time to go down to the station. It's harder to say no to a real person, rather than a voice, isn't it? I need to know that Ric is okay. He's lost his daughter and he doesn't know if he'll ever see her again. They are sure to be treating him like the criminal he's not.

It's time for me to step up as a woman; I thought to myself, as I opened the door to the station, after driving the few blocks in the car. I *saw* Kate this morning. I heard the truth. I saw the pain in her eyes when she recollected her events. It wasn't a game. She didn't *mean* for people to get hurt.

Of course, some truths are best hidden. Kate is gone. Not *physically,* if her plan went as she intended. Telling the police that wouldn't achieve much. If she's dead, then she's an easy target for blame. She can't retaliate. Can't fight back. People will think she won't hurt anyone anymore, now that she's gone. It's better for people to think that that, isn't it? Sometimes, it's better to let go of things, best not to wallow. We can't un-write the past, but we can change the future.

The police station car park was near empty. I let myself in through the large double doors and demanded on the desk to speak with the solicitor - Louise Armstrong. Ric wouldn't be pleased that I went behind his back to see Kate, but there were far more important things for our family to be worrying about now. I was ready to take my own giant leap for mankind.

Chapter Thirty Eight

Alice, 2006

We arrived at the airport in plenty of time. Tom had booked a hire car, which was more like a people carrier than our Peugeot 307. It had already dawned on me that we would have to swap our smaller car for a bigger one sometime in the near future – that three children and their accessories needed a much larger space.

Airport security directed us to a small, private room. We could press a button if we wanted any food or drinks. There was a large, flat-screen TV on the wall. Someone from security came to talk to us. He told us that once the plane landed, Edd and Grace would enter using a VIP system. Their bags wouldn't end up on the usual conveyor. They wouldn't be in the big mass of people that would be disembarking the plane. Reporters were in the arrivals lounge already. We would have more privacy here.

Ethan settled himself by the window. He'd had a long-term obsession with planes. Tom had recently taken him to the British Aviation Museum. He was busy telling Hope the differences in the aircrafts as we saw the plane land. I wondered how long it would take them to get through security.

Tom was sitting, reading some magazine or other, when an official came and told us they were on the way. I wasn't really sure how would to react, what I should say to her? We had discussed calling her by her new name from now on. It seemed the right thing for her; though, to us, she would always be Grace.

Edd walked through the door first, followed by Chloe. It went without saying that she looked just like Hope, though her skin was more tanned and her hair was shorter. Chloe didn't say anything, she looked around at everyone suspiciously, waiting.

"We are so glad you are here with us," I told her. She shrugged her shoulders. We sat down for a moment. I told her briefly about how she had been taken from us, how we had never stopped looking. I told her about her real father, Jack, and the sadness that consumed him after she had gone. Chloe seemed to take it all in, but she didn't comment. I had to refrain from touching her, pulling her into a tight embrace. It's what I expected to happen in my mind for all these years, the day that we would be reunited. I had to console myself that it would take time for her to get to know us, trust us, and love us. That, at the moment, to Chloe, we were the enemy. We had taken her from her quite comfortable life by demanding that she be returned to us.

Hope and Chloe looked at each other with caution. "You're not how I imagined you would be," Hope told her.

Chloe nodded. "I haven't had time to imagine anything, all this – having a twin - having someone who looks just like me. It's a bit strange," Chloe replied. They smiled at each other, with indifference.

Tom picked up her bags as we were led down a VIP stairway and into the car park. We were loading Chloe and Edd's things in the car boot when a reporter managed to sneak his way up to us.

"Grace, are you happy to be back with your family after such an ordeal?" Chloe looked at him with a cold, icy stare. He continued to fire inappropriate questions as we tried to chaperone her into the car.

"Grace, one more thing, do you have anything to say about Richard Sumner - the man who stole you?" He asked. I looked at Edd, then at Tom. The reporter was crossing the line and he knew it. Such a ruthless world in which real people's lives are less significant than the money the papers will make on getting the 'truth' out there on the front page.

"My father," Chloe began, before we could stop her, "is a wonderful man.... As soon as his name is cleared, he's coming to take me home."

The reporter seemed at a loss for words. Edd shoved him out of the way and gave me a glance that I'm sure meant, *'she'll come round.'*

We fastened our seatbelts and Tom started the engine. We began our journey back to Wales. There was no chatter in the car, apart from Edd telling us about how long and tedious the flight had been from LA. No children rejoicing to be with their long-lost sister. I could see Hope was trying to engage with her, catch her eye. Chloe pressed her face permanently at the window as if something, anything, more interesting was happening outside. The next four hours were going to be difficult.

Chapter Thirty Nine

Richard, 2006

The interviews seem to be over. The American Police seem satisfied that I am not a risk to the people of the USA and I'm allowed to leave the Police station. I wanted to rejoice in this fact, but it didn't seem appropriate. I might be free, but there would be people out there that thought I shouldn't be. Jen had posted bail. I wasn't allowed to leave the country until the investigations had finished, couldn't fly straight out there to reclaim my lost daughter. While the police seemed satisfied that I wouldn't be charged in any major way, it would depend on the forgiving nature of the British Police when they went through all of the information.

Louise Armstrong told me that Chloe was now in the UK and under the care of her biological mother, Alice Smith, as she was now called. She seemed confident that we would be allowed to have some contact with her, but it would depend on the goodwill of her 'new' mom, without a court order. She slipped me an address and a phone number for Alice and told me to use it sparingly. They might need time, Louise said. They will want some space at first. I wondered, not for the first time, if they had asked Chloe what *she* wanted. After all, this wasn't all about them, in my mind. It was about Chloe.

Jen was waiting for me in the lobby. She held me and told me that everything would work out, in the end. I wanted to believe her, but I wondered how we were going to fight this - how we were going to get our girl back.

We drove back to the house and it was late at night. I hadn't slept properly in over twenty-four hours. I was exhausted, both mentally and physically. We pulled up in front of the house to find an array of press. I sighed heavily. I must have done something really bad in a previous life to deserve this, I thought. After fighting through the reporters, we managed to get inside. All of the blinds were down. Jen made us some sandwiches. It was decided that her mother would sleep in the spare room until things were sorted out. It would be better for Emily to have someone around to look after her properly while our thoughts were so preoccupied on getting Chloe back.

I started to Google Alice. Tried to find out what kind of a person she is, what kind of mother. I was looking for something that made her look bad, something I could use in a court of law if I had to. I know that sounds awful. I could understand why she wanted her missing daughter back, but I wanted to make her out to be the villain – the family destroyer. The truth was that Kate had managed to do her best at that. I hoped Kate was happy, wherever she was now, with the way she had led our family to the pack of wolves.

I looked at Alice's number again. First thing in the morning, I would make that call to the UK. I'd appeal to her better nature and play nice. I'd have to talk to her about my life, and plead my innocence. I'd have to hope that she had enough compassion to at least let me speak with my daughter. Because, for now, that was the best I was going to get.

Chapter Forty

Chloe, 2006

I used to think that I was an ordinary person. I go to an ordinary school. I live in an ordinary part of town. My grades are nothing extra-ordinary. My life is as typical as any other twelve-year-old American girl. Or, it was, until yesterday.

Suddenly, I'm in a new country. I'm in a car that is full of strangers. *Strangers*. I know that sounds a bit mean; that it isn't what I should be thinking about these new people. Technically, they are my biological family. Alice, Hope, and Ethan anyway. They are the family that I never knew existed. The family that I was stolen from, all those years ago. I'm being taken to a place they all call home, a place I've never been to in my entire life. I'm supposed to just settle down there, go to a new school, and embrace British life. Is it wrong to say that I don't want it? Any of it. These people, the house, the way that passers-by look at me in the street?

It's hard to imagine how my life had been *before*. The police told me that I'd been taken from a pushchair. Stolen. I wasn't made of stone. I felt for Alice, for her family, for what they had been through. I just found it hard to ration that this stolen girl was actually me, that ordinary American girl. That I'd once had a different life with these people. A life I couldn't remember. A life that didn't seem possible.

Jen gave me her phone when I was taken away from my home. I checked it in the bathroom at the airport and it didn't seem to work here. I'll have to ask Alice if we can get the phone looked at. I'll have to wait for the right moment though, wait until I think that she could say yes. It seems strange, having to ask a stranger for permission to do things, having to answer to a new set of rules. Having to fit in somewhere I don't feel like I belong.

Alice and Tom have a nice house, that overlooks the sea. I suppose, in some ways, it's similar to my home with Dad and Jen.

The water won't be as warm, though. We won't see grey whales migrating, or the pods of dolphins. The good thing about the house is that it's quite large, and there seems to be plenty of places that I can disappear. Not literally, of course. They have a dog, Ben, who is an old Labrador. We were never allowed a dog at home. Dad and Jen said they were *too busy* working to be able to take care of a dog properly; that it wouldn't be fair on an animal to be cooped up in the house all day long. Isn't it ironic that now I have one, I don't want it either?

Hope showed me upstairs to my room. It looks out towards the ocean. My room is decorated plainly in pastel colours; but it feels a bit strange, a bit superficial. There is a lavender coloured bedspread and some children's books on a bookshelf. I supposed that if this really was my room, that no one had slept in it before. They had kept it as some kind of living shrine - for the day that I came back.

"You don't remember us, do you?" Hope asked me.

"No," I told her, then added, "Sorry." Hope unnerved me, because we were so similar. It was like looking at a mirror image of myself. Yet, I didn't think we had much in common – how could we? We had lived different lives with different people. I wondered if I would have given her more than a second glance if she had been in one of my classes at school. Probably not.

Hope gestured to a large pile of wrapped gifts in one corner of my new bedroom. I walked over to take a look, peering at the gift tags. *'To Grace, on your fourth birthday'* one of them said, and another: *'Happy Christmas, Grace. 2002.'* I supposed that these were all the presents I had missed over the years, when I should have been Grace. I wondered why Alice had kept them all? Did she think I wouldn't have presents, parties, or Christmases without them? Did they think that the world stopped, that I'd come back one day and be relieved they hadn't forgotten about me?

"It's a bit... strange..." I told Hope. She nodded with understanding.

"I'm not sure I remember you either.... That sounds bad I know. I was so small when you were....." she trailed off, unsure of what word to use, unsure of how to address me without pushing me further away.

"Taken - I suppose that my other mom, Kate, she must have been the one who...took me to a new life...."

"I know it's strange for all of us, now. I know you probably don't like us, for taking you away from your family. I'm not sure if my mum should have let you stay.... It sounds like you had a nice life over there? You were happy?" Hope asked.

"I never had any reason not to be. My mom and dad separated, but that's common now. My step-mom, Jen, she's nice. My sister, Emily, is five...." My mind wondered how Emily would be coping with all of this. She was a shy, little girl who was afraid of change. She wasn't anything like Ethan, my real brother, who hadn't stopped talking all the way here in the car, in an irritating kind of way.

Hope excused herself. I could see that we might become friends, that we were more similar than I thought was possible. I didn't want to think about having to stay here though, in this cold, rainy country. Now that I was over the shock, it didn't even matter to me that Richard wasn't my father, technically. I didn't have one here anyway - no British father to claim me. I wanted to go back. Somehow, I'd find a way.

Chapter Forty One

Alice, 2006

Life was different with Chloe here. The dynamics of the house had shifted. We were all going out of our way to be nice to her, to make her feel welcome. Tom thought we were all going a bit overboard. He said that we were letting her get away with too much. That I didn't ask her to do her share of housework, liked I expected the other two children to do. I didn't ask her to walk the dog, take the bins out. I just let her be.

I suppose I had this image in my mind of some big reunion. We ate last night's dinner mostly in silence. Only Ethan seemed confident enough to ask her questions like: *'What's your favourite aeroplane?'* and *'Do you like sweets or chocolate?'* They were questions that were not going to give us much of an insight to her life. The life she had lived without us.

I left some of our old photo albums lying around the house – in her room, on the kitchen table. I caught her looking at one over breakfast, a picture of Hope and Grace together when they were toddlers. *'We looked happy'* Chloe said in a whisper, followed closely by: *'I don't remember....'* I left her alone with the albums, tried to give her some space to sift through her thoughts without me peering over her shoulder. I tried not to crowd her.

The school head-teacher called to say there was a place for Grace, when she was ready. I told her that we were calling her Chloe, for the moment. That maybe in a couple of weeks she might be ready to take that next step, ready to take on her proper identity. That she seemed resistant to living her life here, with us. I found that to be the hardest part of having her home. Hearing the little snippets of *'I'll be going home soon'* and *'I'm not going to be here for long.'* It was sad, and I didn't have the heart to tell her that she was wrong. We had spent ten years looking for her, and there was no way I could go through losing her *again*.

The information about her kidnapping was still being filtered through from the USA. It could take a couple of weeks until we had all the information. We had been informed that Richard Sumner had been released on bail. They had found the wreckage of her mother's car by the sea, and they were now looking for her body. I didn't tell Chloe that though, I couldn't. I wasn't entirely sure what kind of relationship she had had with Kate Sumner. Edd told me that Chloe had been living with Richard and Jen for the last couple of years, that contact with her 'mother' had been minimal.

I received calls from well-wishers; from people I trusted enough to be given my mobile number, because Tom had unplugged the landline as soon are we arrived back from the airport. Mary, the family liaison officer who saw me through some difficult times in Cornwall in those mid-to-late 90s, sent kind words. The missing people's website sent us flowers. I made a mental note to call them and ask them for advice on how to help Chloe settle in.

At some point, I'd have to make contact with Richard Sumner - find out what kind of person he really was, how he had managed to bring up a girl without knowing she didn't belong to him. Tom encouraged me to put it off, to make contact through the proper channels – solicitors, lawyers. '*He has no rights,*' he told me. I knew he was right. I knew I should let it go. But I also knew that I lived for all those years without knowing that my daughter was actually safe, and loved. At the very least, didn't I owe him that? Didn't I owe him thanks, for everything he had done for Chloe? Could I wish such a thing on someone else - the not knowing if she is okay? Even if that someone was who I thought was my worst enemy?

I began clearing away the breakfast dishes and started loading them into the sink. I'd have to try to break the ice with Chloe today. I'd have to find some way to tell her the truth, that she wouldn't be going home to the Sumners. I was thinking about how difficult it was going to be, when my mobile phone rang. I answered on the third ring.

"Hello?" I said.

"Is this Alice?" a voice asked. It seemed far away, distant.

"Yes," I said, unsure of who I was talking to. I didn't want to be talking to anyone at the moment. I had to be on my guard for reporters, and people wanting information about Chloe. I wanted to keep the press at bay for a little longer. Of course, we would have to make a statement to the press at some point today, but for now that could wait.

"This is Richard Sumner..." the voice began, "We need to talk...."

Chapter Forty Two

Richard, 2006

Straight after breakfast I decided I needed to call the UK. I was going through torture - the not knowing if she was okay. The not knowing if they were looking after her, treating her properly. Wondering what they were telling her and if they were using underhand tactics to make her think that she didn't matter to us anymore.

Louise Armstrong was going to fight the conditions of my bail. It was a long shot, but without the ban on travel being lifted, there was nothing I could do. I felt hopeless. It could take up to a couple of weeks to get the ban lifted, if it was even possible. Normally, a couple of weeks would seem like nothing - the time would pass us by before we knew it. This time, however, I knew that every second without Chloe would count. That every day I woke up in the morning, I'd have to realise I couldn't do what I wanted to do – to fly to the UK and bring her home.

Jen and I talked about Alice before I made the call. Emily was being dropped off at kindergarten by Jen's mother. Jen told me that I had to think like a woman. Think about what she had lost for all the years that Chloe was with us. All those Christmases and birthdays. It shocked me to hear that if we didn't do this right, the shoe would be firmly on the other foot. That the people missing out on all those special occasions would be us. It was unimaginable.

I dialled the number and it rang a few times before she answered. I told her that it was me and the line when silent. Silent for too long.

"I'm not sure that I have anything to say to you," she eventually responded.

"I know you think what I did was wrong. But I had no idea. No idea, at all, that Chloe was anything less than my daughter....Please, we just need to know if she is okay, and how she is holding out. Maybe even, we could speak to her?" I asked her cautiously.

"Oh, she's great," she said in a sarcastic tone. "She's being forced to live with people she has never met; in a country that she hasn't set foot in since she was two years old. We aren't the perpetrators of this *crime,* but that's what it feels like for us - every time she talks about going home, to you, to the people she loves. Maybe it would have been better for her to have been ill-treated for all that time, because at least she might have some gratitude, some compassion."

"Please, Alice. Let's not argue. We need to move forward. We need to find a way for this to work for all of us. This isn't the answer. This isn't what's best for Chloe in the long term..." I let my voice trail off and paused. I wanted her to realise that we were the victims too.

"Her name is Grace," she continued assertively. "What Grace needs right now is space. You calling up here, demanding to speak with her, isn't going to make the situation any better for her. You're only going to make it worse. I'll speak to our solicitor and ask her advice on this matter. Until then, please don't call back. We will call you if we decide that is the way forward. Grace is back where she belongs and that's where she is going to stay."

The line went dead.

Chapter Forty Three

Edd, 2006

It was interesting to be an observer to the goings on in the Smith household over the next few days. In some ways, tensions became less intense, but in others, they seemed to have heightened. We released a press statement, which satisfied the press, at least for now. I made an additional statement about Alan. Nothing had happened there yet, but no news is good news, isn't it?

Chloe became more like herself. She seemed to bond well with Ethan, but she also kept the adults and her sister at arm's length. She didn't make any demands; she was simply there. I tried to help her fix her phone, but I suspected the problem was in the using of it abroad. I told her she would have to ask Alice or Tom, to which she frowned. The biggest problem for Chloe was that she missed her family. We weren't just talking about a little bit of being homesickness, she genuinely missed them.

World War Three had erupted over dinner a couple of days ago. Alice was rattled by a phone call from Richard Sumner. Chloe became quite upset and angry that she wasn't allowed to speak with him. Alice lashed out, to which Chloe just stood up and walked away, calmly, to her room. I was the buffer, the 'go between'. The irony hadn't escaped me that a few days ago Chloe barely wanted to talk to me at all.

How do you get over such a devastating tragedy? I could see this one from both sides -from Alice being the victim all those years ago, and to Chloe being the victim now, forced into a life that she didn't want. There would have to be some real concessions on both sides for everyone to be able to move forward without too much ill-feeling. Alice couldn't bear the thought that Chloe was desperate for contact with her father. Desperate to be with people who caused Alice so much pain. Again, it was quite understandable, but how do you express all of this to a child? A child who just wants her old life back.

Richard was in the process of fighting his bail. I spoke to an old friend who was a lawyer, and he seemed to think that Richard stood a good chance. I certainly believed that once the bail was lifted he would be over here faster than the speed of light - trying to see Chloe; trying to make it right.

Kate's body was still missing. There had been some bad rain and winds the night after her car was found. There was talk of her being dragged further out to sea by the stronger-than-usual currents. Something about her did not seem quite right. Not *her,* but the situation. It seemed highly suspicious to me. Highly convenient that she was now missing and presumed dead.

Tom hired a cottage in the Lake District for a long weekend - one of those cottages that were on a long road to nowhere. He thought a change of scene would do everyone some good. That some 'quality family time' would make a difference. I agreed to go along, for Chloe really. Her face seemed so desperate, that I couldn't see how she would really have any fun. I'd talk to her about moving forward. I'd talk to talk to Alice too. Ethan was becoming a little monkey while all of this was going on. It was typical of children to feel left out when the world revolved around someone else. Ethan needed to be reeled back in before the situation got worse, before he made a real cry for attention.

I went upstairs to my room and started to gather some things. I'd not been to the Lake District for some time, but my memory definitely remembered it as a very wet place, no matter what the season. I often wondered how people managed to live there - all year round. How they managed without all the things that we often take for granted by living in suburbia – the shops being the main thing.

Thinking about what I needed, I barely heard my mobile phone ring. I answered it.

"Edward Harper?"

"Yes, that's me," I replied

"I saw your plea on the news. We have a man here, around the same age as your brother, Alan. He came to us in... unusual circumstances. He has interesting memories of a brother named Edd and a happy life with his family. It goes against everything we have on record for him, so we all thought he was making up these stories.....So I wonder, if you could come out to us? I've spoken to the duty manager and she's happy to go ahead with DNA testing. You can meet James; see what you think?"

My mind was buzzing. Could this really be happening? So soon too, after the press conference. Could it really be true that this man, with a mysterious past, is Alan? I had to go. I knew that, instantly. I had no choice; I had to know.

"Where are you?" I asked the woman.

"Just outside of Carlisle," she replied. I did some quick mental calculations - I could be there in a few hours. I could be looking at my brother soon afterwards.

"I'll be there. Give me a couple of hours? I'm currently in Wales...."

"That will be fine."

"What's the postcode?" She gave it to me and I wrote it down on the back of a receipt from the airport.

"I'll see you soon then. I didn't catch your name...."

"Sarah," she filled in. "We will be waiting for you."

Chapter Forty Four

Kate, 2006

It has been a week since I was killed in the car accident. I use the term loosely of course, because I am still very much alive, very much living. I've been driving around in my van, trying to catch the news, staying in deserted lay-by's and trying not to draw too much attention to myself. The papers have come down hard on Ric and Jen. Much harder than I had anticipated and hoped. From what I could understand, Ric was fighting the conditions of his bail, but it was going to be an uphill struggle. He wanted to get out to England as soon as possible to be with our daughter, to give her the support and love she needed. He always had been a good father.

I'd booked a flight that left for the UK without too many changes. Security didn't scrutinise my new passport, didn't give it more than a second glance as I got ready to board my plane. They didn't seem bothered by me wanting to travel, alone, to England, didn't ask *why*. I managed to pick up another van quite easily, hired from a rental company near the airport. They seemed perplexed about my need for a camper van and not some state of the art estate car. I told them I wanted to hit the road and tour the country that I wanted to see places that were *off the beaten track*. It was a half-truth; it *was* in a way what I would be doing in a manner of speaking. But then, I could hardly shout from the rooftops about the *real* reason I was here. The authorities would have me in jail faster than you could say the word 'go'.

I drove steadily up to Wales, stopping at a couple of service stations on the way, and then across to the Isle of Anglesey. I checked in at Kingsbridge Caravan Park, which wasn't too far from the Smith's house, just outside Beaumaris. I'd have to be careful not to get too close to Chloe. My disguise might fool the rest of the world, but she was a bright girl; she would know in an instant that I was here. Eventually, I'd have to make my presence known to her, but not now. Not until I had weighed up the situation for all it was worth.

I drove slowly past the house, which was set back just off the road, overlooking the sea. It reminded me a little of the place where Ric and Jen lived now – quaint and unspoiled. I didn't see Chloe, but I did see a young boy playing with a black dog in the garden. There were three cars in the drive, and there were definitely people in the house. I pulled over in a lay-by and walked back along the road. I'd bought a good pair of binoculars back in the States and I was sure I would be able to see the people clearly through the windows with them.

I focused first on the downstairs room facing me. Alice was in there with Tom, and it looked like they were talking while preparing something for dinner. I moved to a room upstairs, that was painted in pastel colours. Chloe was sitting at her desk, typing something on her computer. I wondered if the Smiths allowed her to maintain contact with Ric. She looked healthy enough, but glum. She'd always been a daddy's girl. This would be very hard on her.

I couldn't bear to watch her from such a distance - with such detachment. I decided to head back to the caravan park to get an early night's sleep and come back first thing in the morning. I would wait until there was an opportunity for me to present myself to her. Alice didn't strike me as a mother who wrapped a child in cotton wool, or as a mother who liked to be in control at all times. Sooner or later I'd get my chance. Chloe needed to know the truth. She needed familiarity, to know that despite everything, she was loved. I failed her by bringing her to a different country and passing her off as my own. This time I was going to make it right.

Chapter Forty Five

Alice, 2006

Chloe had been home with us for nearly a week when I decided that we would take a weekend break as a family. It had been a tough time for us all. Harder than I ever anticipated. I'll admit that I expected gratitude from my daughter, expected her to be happy at being reunited with her long-lost family. Instead, all I seem to have managed to do is upset her – by bringing her here, by not letting her talk on the phone with her father.

I knew I was going to have to have a serious talk with Chloe - about her future, about her other family. I couldn't even begin to consider the terms Richard Sumner's lawyer had sent over *'A mutual agreement which has Chloe's best interests at heart'* – that's what she called it. I couldn't begin to see how I could seriously consider giving them more access to my daughter after the ten years of nothing we had received.

Information was now coming to light that Richard's ex-wife had taken Grace after suddenly losing her own daughter. She had taken Grace from her pushchair that morning, and managed to pass her off as her own daughter. While I could see that, perhaps, it wasn't Richards's actions that led to our loss, I couldn't help but harbour ill feeling towards him. Surely, he must have known on some level, that something wasn't right?

Hope and Chloe were getting along well, all things considered. They would walk to the beach together in the afternoons and I'd watch them from the top window, laughing, and playing. It was the only time I saw Chloe happy. The only time she let her guard down – when she thought she wasn't being watched. I was glad that they had managed to be themselves with each other after all those years of separation. I thought about Hope; she had come a long way from the mute toddler she had become after her sister was taken.

Edd had taken a strange call from a woman who ran a care home in north Cumbria. She had seen Edd's plea on the television the previous day and wondered if she should act on her suspicions. I was relieved that she had been watching and had the guts to make the call. Relieved that someone else might have some closure - at least. Edd had done so much for our family; he deserved his own family back. I just hoped this woman was genuine and wasn't leading him on a false trail. That Edd would have the ending to Alan's disappearance that he wanted. We had arranged for him to join us after his meeting; he would be popping over to the northeast to see his mam either way. I just hoped that if this man was Alan, they would have a more satisfactory reunion than we'd had.

Tom loaded our things into the car the night before we left. He liked things to be organised. He didn't like last minute packing, last minute holidays. He wanted to know what we were taking, what we needed, what time we were stopping. As much as I loved him, he was the last person you would ever want to take on a serious road trip. It would be his idea of hell, and my idea of torture.

The girls packed their things by themselves, while I helped Ethan choose between what he wanted to take and what he really needed. Six-year-old boys were a challenge, and I often felt that Ethan was trying to push my buttons. He was much more demanding than his sister had been when they were younger. Hope had never been as argumentative as a child. You could have taken her anywhere and you would have barely noticed her presence. She was a watcher and a listener, while Ethan was more like a bull in a china shop.

It would only take us a few hours to reach the Lake District, straight up the M6 and then onto the main road that ran through the national park – of which Tom dutifully informed me there was only one. We were staying in a cottage that was just outside of Coniston - Tilberthwaite they called it. It was a hamlet with only a few houses. Close enough to amenities if we needed them, but otherwise, we would be able to do what we liked without being too disturbed by other people. Tom had packed board games and books. Ethan had packed his DS. I hoped the girls would be a bit more willing to engage in family time.

I had no doubts that this trip would make or break us. It would mark the beginning or the end of our lives as a family of five. If only I could have known what would follow...

Chapter Forty Six

Kate, 2006

I tried to keep away from the Smith's house that night, but I couldn't. My motherly instinct was too strong. I couldn't risk the thought that I might get my moment to speak with Chloe, an opportunity that I'd miss by sitting alone in my van with my thoughts. So I took the van and went back.

There was a lot more movement in the house this evening, which seemed strange. Tom was loading up a car, as if they were taking some kind of trip. Bags were loaded into the boot, one by one. I saw Chloe come out with her sister, putting their bags in the back of the people carrier before going straight back inside again. The resemblance was remarkable. Not that it should be such a surprise to me; I had known from early on, soon after I'd taken her, that she had an identical twin.

I decided there and then that I wouldn't be going back to the campsite this evening. I'd hide my van a bit further down the road in a passing place - the road they would have to follow if they were planning to leave Anglesey. I had a bad feeling about this trip they were taking. A bad feeling that something wasn't quite right.

I was going to follow them.

Chapter Forty Seven

Edd, 2006

I reached the care home a lot quicker than I'd anticipated. I stopped somewhere on the M6 for a sandwich and a coffee. I thought about what I remembered about Alan – his love of comics and chocolate bars. I wondered how he had ended up there in the care home? Alan was two years younger than I was, which put him in his early fifties now. I thought about what the woman, Sarah, had told me on the phone. They had thought that the things he remembered were a lie. Why would anyone think that? What kind of problems did they think that James had?

As I continued to drive north, I thought about my mother. She would be ecstatic to know that this *could* be Alan. The trouble was, that I didn't have the heart to lift her spirits so high and then bring them crashing back down if he wasn't our Alan. Until I knew for certain, she would have to wait. I hoped that it wouldn't be long.

I found the home easily, and pulled the car into the elaborate car park. It didn't look like your average run of the mill care home, that much was evident. The gardens were large and elaborate - well maintained and cared for, probably by a full-time gardener. The building itself looked more like the stately home of a millionaire than a place to hold people who had mental problems. Some of the residents seemed quite happy sitting on the terrace, drinking tea and eating cakes. They didn't look sad or angry, didn't have any outwardly obvious problems. I knocked on the door and waited.

Sarah came towards it, friendly and welcoming. She took me into a side room as she explained some of the 'problems' they had had with James. He had come to them from another centre, where he had been aggressive towards an older man. The reason for the aggression was not completely unknown. James had originally been found in an abandoned warehouse with other children. It housed a paedophile ring that used the children for providing services to the older men. James was one of the few children who had been left behind. Since then, he'd lived with foster carers, and the father had been quite violent with quite a temper, which was when James started exhibiting these 'hallucinations' and 'flashbacks' from his early childhood. At sixteen, they moved him to a secure juvenile centre for young adults with mental health problems. He had been shifted around various other 'homes' ever since.

I felt sad, when I listened to his story, of the life he had lived without us. If only the government had listened to my mother, then none of these problems would exist. If only they had listened. Sarah told me they hadn't told James I was coming. They wanted to see if he had a reaction to me, to see if he really did remember his previous life, his previous family. I thought briefly about Alice and Chloe – Grace had been two years old when she had been abducted; she had no recollection of her life before, nothing at all. Would James be any different? At eight, surely he was old enough to remember with certainty the life he had been taken from?

Sarah took me through to one of the main day rooms. It was light and airy, painted magnolia with a variety of dark-brown, soft leather sofas. Sarah gestured to the man in the chair by the window. He was focused on a book, absorbed in its pages. Sarah held back and let me take the lead. I strode towards the table and I sat in the chair beside him.

As he looked up at me, his eyes changed from that of bewilderment to that of wonder. He smiled.

"You've changed a lot, Edward," he said to me.

I nodded, suddenly completely lost for words. This man wasn't the young boy who left us, the boy that my mind remembered, but I could see in his face that he was one and the same.

"It's about bloody time you got yourself here, though. Where've you been, all these years?" he asked.

"Looking for you," I replied. It was the truth; we had never stopped looking. Mam said she never would, not until someone actually gave her his body. That he was still out there, somewhere, waiting to be found. That's partly why I had carried on for so long. I wanted her to have peace, to know. I didn't want her to die, as an old lady, with all of it on her shoulders.

James stood up. He held out his hand and then decided a full on embrace would be more appropriate. We stood there, as if all those years hadn't mattered. As if nothing had changed between us at all.

"Alan," I said to him. "It's time to go home."

Chapter Forty Eight

Kate, 2006

They had travelled north to the Lake District, to a place that was so deserted it was hard to avoid being spotted. I kept far back on that winding, narrow road to the cottage. I stopped just shy of the last bend where I watched them unload and go inside. I decided there was only one thing to do – abandon my camper van further away, and watch them as often as I could on foot. Possibly, the only good thing about the cottage was that it was surrounded by dense woodland. It would make hiding quite easy, so long as I didn't attract too much attention to myself, so long as I was careful.

The first day they went out somewhere in the car. On the second day they mostly stayed close to the cottage, the children playing outside in the wide, open garden. Tom lit a BBQ early in the evening. Two men appeared and they seemed to be having some kind of celebration of sorts. I thought I recognised one of the men from the newspapers as the private detective who had found Chloe - Edd something - but I couldn't be sure.

Hope was mixing with the adults while the boy edged closer and closer to the woods. I'd wandered around them quite extensively the day before; they went on for miles and eventually you came to an unused quarry. The edges were very steep and dropped into a pool - of what I suspected to be - very deep water. There seemed to be an opening into some kind of cave. I never went into it though, dark places hadn't been my thing since I was a little child. They reminded me too much of the horrors that came in the night.

As the evening wore on, the adults seemed to be having what I would describe as - a jolly old time. The children were being less and less observed. Hope had gone inside the house some time before. The boy was still near the woods. Chloe was watching, listening – edging slightly closer to where the boy was when she thought he wasn't looking. She always had been a watcher as a child - quiet but watchful. You couldn't do anything without her noticing. It used to drive Ric mad.

Suddenly, the boy bolted. He ran as fast as his little legs would allow him, like a cheetah hunting its prey. Chloe watched, waited, walked quietly out of view from the adults, and followed him. It took me less than a split-second to decide that I had to follow her, that whatever these two were up to, it was clearly no good. Unbeknown to the little boy, if he ran far enough, he would end up in a very dangerous place.

Chapter Forty Nine

Alice, 2006

The weekend was going much better than I had anticipated. The cottage was cosy, as opposed to luxurious. It had a homely feel to it and reminded me quite a bit of my old house in Perranporth. I made a mental note to try to take Chloe and Hope back there sometime soon – to see if it jogged Chloe's memory at all, see if it would help her to remember us. Chloe and Hope had to share a twin room and I tried not to feel too bad about it. They had been getting along well, after all. It was *normal* for sisters to share.

We took the car over to Hawkshead on the first day, went inside Beatrix Potter's house, and ate lunch in a little cafe that sold enormous slices of cake. Ethan, a great lover of Peter Rabbit, was enthralled. The twins were much less amused. Later, we wandered to Coniston, took a boat that went for a little sail on the lake. The Lake District was a beautiful place in the right weather, but I imagined it would be hell in those winter months when the snow closed all the narrow country lanes and the supermarket was miles and miles away. Still, I, above all people, knew that humans were resilient things. They can cope with far more than you think.

On the second day, we stayed at the house mostly, we wandered into the woods a little and didn't really do a lot. We played some board games in the living room for a short time after lunch. Ethan and Chloe were good at occupying themselves in the garden. Tom and Hope had gone to find supplies for a BBQ that evening – sausages and bread rolls.

I'd spoken with Edd on the phone the day before, and it turned out that James was in fact his missing brother. He'd been sectioned under the mental health act for his 'illusions' about his past, and his insistence of a happy life he had once led, that on paper never existed. Some strings had been pulled, but Edd wasn't going to leave James in the place a moment longer than necessary. Though, he did insist that it was the best care home he had ever been inside.

The two brothers travelled straight over to the northeast where Alan was happily reunited with his mother. The plan was for them to drive over the following evening and join us in a joint kind of celebration.

So, that is how we found ourselves - that night: Drinking wine in the garden with friends, talking to James about his experiences in the place where Edd had found him, talking about what we had gone through to find Grace.

I can't quite remember what time it was, when I realised that Ethan and Chloe were nowhere to be seen. I had a vague recollection of them playing just near the woods. It was amazing how such a happy, jolly situation could become very sober and dry in only a matter of seconds. Tom, Edd, and James all set off in different directions, shouting, looking. I called the local police.

My memory flashed back to that day in 1996, the first time we lost Grace. Surely, this couldn't be happening *again?* The men returned from their search, but there was no sign of the missing children. The police had called for backup officers to come from another nearby village. The mountain rescue brought sniffer dogs. For such a small, desolate community, I was surprised at the thoroughness of the emergency services. Surprised at how much they cared, as the night started to draw darker.

As I sat, waiting, I knew I needed to call Richard Sumner. He had a right to know that Chloe was missing. A right to know that we had failed her, *again*. I called the number in the USA and he answered on the second ring.

"Hello?" he said in a sleepy voice. I hadn't spared a thought to the time difference. It seemed so inconsequential, given the circumstances.

"Richard? It's Alice..." I began, "I'm phoning to.... well.... I'm calling because I think that you should know...we've lost her...Chloe. She's just... completely *disappeared*"

I was unable to elaborate any further. My body broke down in loud, uncontrollable sobs. I vaguely remember Tom picking up the phone, trying to calm Richard down. Telling him we would call back as soon as there was any news. Telling him not to worry, not to panic. It was no good though. I knew that any good parent would be thinking all of those things. Richard Sumner would be in pieces until his daughter was found.

We had to find the children before the real darkness set in. It couldn't end like this; I wouldn't let it. I wouldn't tolerate the idea of the children being out there, alone in the woods. Chloe may not like us all that much, she may not like the new life that had been forced upon her, but I resolved, there and then that once all of this was over, once we had them back in the safety of our little cottage, we would do whatever it took to make it right.

Chapter Fifty

Chloe, 2006

I followed Ethan into the depths of the woods. Close enough to see where he was running, but far enough back so I wasn't seen. He began to slow after about thirty minutes. I wondered if he knew where he was going? It was starting to get dark. I wasn't sure that I could find my way back to the house even if I wanted to.

We must have been on the move for nearly an hour, when Ethan looked sharply to his left and froze. I turned my glance to the place he was looking and I could see a medium-sized figure in dark clothes, cowering behind a tree. Watching. Waiting. I suddenly realised that we were being followed, but didn't have time to begin to wonder why, when Ethan bolted straight ahead of him. I ran faster to keep up with him, to try to make him realise that he wasn't as alone in the woods as he thought.

His little legs kept moving, and in the semi-darkness - at the exact spilt second I realised he was going to run off some kind of edge. I watched him completely disappear.

*

As I walked carefully towards the edge, I could hear Ethan crying for his mum - our mother, I should say. Alice. I moved slowly to the edge and, lying on my stomach, I looked down. He had landed on a very small ledge, four feet or so down. Clutching his right arm in pain, he was sobbing softly. Below him was another fifty feet of sheer drop, and a large pool of water – that I guessed, in the middle, would be about a hundred metres deep. I looked to my right and saw the sign: *'unfenced rock faces and very deep water'*. There was no way that Ethan could climb from where he was with a bad arm. Yet, there was also no way the tiny ledge that was crumbling beneath him, was going to last much longer.

"Ethan, look up, it's me – Chloe," I shouted. He looked up towards me, his face showing some sign of relief.

"Someone's been watching us, watching the house. A bad man..." he began to tell me.

"Don't worry about the bad man, Ethan. I'm going to help you. You need to keep very still, I'm going to come down to you. We are going to try to move over. Look - see the other ledge?"

Ethan looked to his right, to the larger, slightly more stable ledge. Surely, someone must have noticed we were missing by now; surely people were out somewhere nearby looking for us?

"I can't move; it's too scary," he told me.

"Ethan, if you don't move you'll fall. If you fall off that ledge you're going to hit the rocks and die. If you're really lucky you might fall in the water, but you're not going to be able to swim with a busted arm....It's getting darker. We need to do this very quickly..."

As I let my words sink in I heard the rustle of footsteps behind me. In all the commotion, I'd forgotten about the person who had been following us, forgotten that we were still probably being followed.

The figure walked calmly towards me and I was struck by the familiarity of the persons size and shape. My brain clicked into gear and I knew instantly who it was, and felt relief, relief that we would be ok.

"Mom?" I whispered.

Chapter Fifty One

Kate, 2006

I never planned for our reunion to be like this, in such dire circumstances. I knew that I couldn't stay in the shadows and watch my daughter try to save her brother. That putting the children before myself was the only available option. The drop was too steep and too risky for children to attempt to conquer by themselves.

Alice and Tom hadn't spoken about me to Chloe since she had arrived in the UK. Chloe told me she'd been looking at the US news on her laptop. She thought I was gone. I told her that none of that mattered at the moment. What I did was terribly wrong, but it didn't make me love her any less.

"You can't go down there, Chloe - it's far too dangerous..." I told her. I looked around. A climbing rope had been slung over the branch of a nearby tree – left assumedly by some climber or other. I tugged at the rope – it seemed safe. We didn't really have any option other than to trust its durability. I double tied the rope around the trunk of the tree, which was the most secure thing we had. I made a make shift harness around Chloe's tiny body – knotting with figure of eights.

"I'm going to go down there... that ledge to the right is a little more stable. I can raise Ethan up to you; you'll have to grab him by both arms. Don't worry about the break. It'll hurt him, but at least he'll be alive at the end of it. You'll have to pull yourselves back up to the edge...help will be coming... Alice and Tom are good people. You just wait here; don't try to move him. Wrap yourselves in my jacket."

Chloe nodded assertively. Ethan continued to whimper. I didn't have to tell Chloe that I'd probably not make it back up myself, that lifting Ethan would put strain on the rocks beneath me and it would likely crumble at my feet. I began to descend carefully as she watched me, wide-eyed, lying on her stomach near the edge, with the rope securely tied around her.

I made my way slowly down to Ethan, and it was hard work. I'd never been a climber, never been awfully good at balancing myself. When I reached the edge next to him, I told him to move cautiously towards me, one step at a time. As he stepped over to my ledge - with help - I felt it begin to crumble beneath me. We had only one chance to get this right.

"Chloe, are you ready? This ledge isn't very secure, you need to be ready to grab Ethan as soon as I lift him up. Okay?"

"Okay, I'm ready," she replied.

I lifted him up as fast as I dared. I watched as Chloe grabbed both of his hands tightly. I was going to have to jump to push him high enough for her to be able to lift him to the safety of the other side. He was lower than I thought, even with me lifting him. Without a push, Chloe would never manage to pull him up to the other side.

I counted to three. I jumped with all my might, propelling him upwards. As I landed back down on the ledge, I had a split-second before the rocks started to collapse. I closed my eyes. I let myself fall.

Chapter Fifty Two

Chloe, 2006

I managed to lift Ethan over the edge and we shuffled back to safety. I listened to the rocks crashing downwards, and my mom hitting the bottom with a loud thud. I didn't have the strength to look down, but I knew that she was gone. I didn't have too much time to dwell on it though - I had to take care of Ethan

Ethan was clinging to me, and I managed to move us further back to the tree, wrapping my mom's jacket around us both. We sat in stunned silence.

"Your other mum saved my life," he told me. I nodded, glumly.

"She's going to be the hero now," he added.

I thought about my mom, about the life she had lived. The choices she had made that had taken us to this moment. I knew that people didn't like her for what she had done, but I also knew that she had been made to look like someone she was not – a real criminal.

I thought about Ethan's words to me and realised that he was right. She had died a hero. She had died in a selfless act to save a child that she barely knew. She couldn't undo what she had done in her past, but she had saved a child's future.

It didn't matter to me anymore, the reasons why she had taken me. It wouldn't matter if I stayed in England until I was old enough to choose otherwise. I knew that my real heart belonged in America, with my father.

Our mothers are the ones who define us, who help us grow. Our mothers are the ones who love us unconditionally, the ones who try to give us a better life. In the most bizarre set of circumstances, I'd been blessed with a wonderful mother. I'd find my way in life and I'd never forget her. Maybe I could learn to like Alice, the woman who had given me life, but my spirit would be with Kate, always.

Chapter Fifty Three

Alice, 2006

They were found near the edge of a disused quarry, holding each other beneath a tree. Ethan was taken straight to the hospital in an ambulance. He had broken his arm badly in two places. Chloe was fine; physically, at least. She told us how she'd followed Ethan into the woods and watched him fall over the edge; how her mother had emerged from the woods behind her and sacrificed her life to save my son.

The police had cordoned off the quarry, and her body was removed by experts, zipped in a body bag, and carried out on a stretcher. The press were everywhere, and we decided that the best thing to do, after a night in a hotel, was to go back to Wales.

It's hard to accept that someone you had thought of as the villain was capable of such a good deed, but that's what I did over those next few days. Chloe was more settled with us now, more tolerant of being part of our family. But I knew really, in my heart of hearts, that the kindest thing to do for her, the most loving thing, would be to send her home, to the family she had grown up with.

I'd battled with it, griped with it. Tried to make myself think that she could be happy here with us permanently – but it was no good. It always came back to the same thing: As much as I loved her, I had to let her go, or else, she would resent me forever. I had to let her go in the hope that, one day, when she was ready, she would accept me as her mother.

Richard Sumner was ecstatic when I called him to tell him the news. I told him we wanted to maintain regular contact – that we would have to discuss birthdays, Christmases, and school holidays. I told him I had spent ten years not knowing if she was safe, well, and loved. Ten years of wonder. I could send her back knowing that she was out there, at the end of a phone. Knowing that she was living a good life with people who genuinely loved her. I knew they would take good care of my daughter.

We hadn't told Chloe that the bail conditions had been revoked and the arrangements were set. That her family would be flying over to England to sign all the necessary paperwork in order for it to happen.

I asked her to go and answer the door while I busied myself in the kitchen, as I tried to step back and let them have this moment. I heard her squeals of delight at opening the door to her past - her family, standing there before her. I saw the tears of happiness that fell from her face, and I knew without any reservations that I was doing the right thing.

After dinner, we sat her down and told her.

"Thank you," she said through mixed emotions. The adults in the room raised their glasses in toast.

"To the future," Chloe said.

Chapter Fifty Four

Richard, 2006

We buried Kate on a Tuesday in a small ceremony with those who knew her. The sun was shining and the birds sang. It was a beautiful day - the best kind of day to say goodbye. Chloe coped remarkably well with the loss of her mother – she arranged the flowers and the hymns all by herself. We had the remains of the real Chloe buried alongside her. It didn't seem right that they should be separate. It seemed fitting that, in the end, they would be together at last.

We focused on celebrating Kate's life, rather than wallowing in our own self-pity. The church was full of flowers sent by strangers, people who were touched by her self-sacrifice, by her ability to make things right. It was, I believed, the way it should be. She was now able to rest in peace.

Jen and I spent a lot of time working out the legalities of moving forward from here with the Smith's lawyers. The main thing for us was keeping Chloe as Chloe, in a more legal capacity, and changing her surname to Sumner-Smith, which would give her a strong foothold in both households. Chloe would never come to accept being called Grace, not when she had grown up as Chloe. Understandably, the Smiths wanted to stay in regular contact with their daughter, which we completely understood. We needed to work together now to ensure that Chloe had the best of everything in life with all her family.

When the day came for us to return to California, Chloe was faced with mixed emotions. She had developed a strong bond with her new siblings and came to realise that Alice wasn't the monster she had first perceived. For many years, the tabloids had called Grace, 'The Missing Half'. We had come full circle. Grace was no longer missing, she was now part of a whole – a whole world of opportunities that awaited her.

We waved our goodbyes from the aeroplane door, and we took the first step, together, as a family.

Epilogue: One Year Later

Chloe, 2007

It's been a year since I was found. A year since my world was ripped apart, and a year since it was sewn back together.

Although the pain of losing my mom is still with me, I'm able to look back on my childhood with mostly good memories - without too much sadness. Mostly, I am grateful for the life I have been given, because back in 1996, on the day I was taken, I could have ended up anywhere, with anyone. Ethan calls them *bad people*. You could argue that I wouldn't have been taken at all, I suppose. But I was, and this was my story.

We are sitting now in our garden in California. All my family - new and old - together. The sun is shining and the weather is warm. Ethan and Emily play happily in the pool, splashing around. All of my parents are standing chatting away, happily. It feels right. It feels perfect.

I've spent quite a bit of time over in Wales in the last year, and I have begun to have a new relationship with my biological mother, with Alice. I'm not sure that I'll ever be able to replace my mother with her, but I am sure our relationship will blossom with more time. Alice is still working part-time at the zoo but they still do a lot of fundraising for missing children, for all those children who are still out there, waiting to be found. She wants to make sure that people don't stop looking, that help and support is there for them when they need it - particularly with families who are reunited with their children after many years of separation. They know first-hand that it isn't plain sailing. They want others to be able to find peace and move on.

Edd is still looking for missing people, but he doesn't work as much as he used to – when he was looking for me. He's been dating the girl he met at the nursing home, Sarah, and he seems happier, at peace. James still has problems related to his past, but he is having counselling in order to deal with his feelings. Their mother died in her sleep six months after they were all reunited. Edd told us that she'd been able to let herself go since finding Alan. That she was at peace now knowing that he was safe.

Me? I'm still finding my place in the world. Finding how best to fit in at all the different places I now live, trying just to be a normal kid. It doesn't matter where life takes you or how difficult the paths might be. I remind myself every day that when life gives you a hundred reasons to cry, you have to show life you have a thousand reasons to smile.

THE END

About the Author

Brooke is a mother, hen keeper, teacher, PA, and private tutor. In her spare time you'll usually find her swimming in a lake or riding over a mountain on her bike. She drinks a lot of tea, likes books, and loves cake.

Brooke lives in the Lake District with her family.

"The Missing Half" is her first novel.

To find out more visit www.brookepowley.com

Printed in Great Britain
by Amazon.co.uk, Ltd.,
Marston Gate.